Fay Wentworth and her family live in Herefordshire. She has pursued her love of creative writing through a career, marriage and motherhood. Her stories for children and adults have been published in a variety of magazines and placed in several competitions. Her recently published book, *Chase a Rainbow*, can be found in libraries. This is her first collection of short stories

To Jasmine
Best wishes, Fay (Wentworth)
Swanwick 2011

Destiny's Footprints

A collection of short stories

Fay Wentworth

Published by
Butford Publishing Ltd.
Hall Farm, Birlingham, Pershore, Worcs. WR10 3AB

Photography: Hugh Morris

First published 2009

Copyright © 2009 Fay Wentworth

British Library Cataloguing in Publication Data
A catalogue record for this book is available from the British Library

ISBN 978-0-9552474-3-9

4 / 2.1.1

Printed in Great Britain by
HSW Print, Tonypandy, Rhondda

Contents

Acknowledgements

Thanks to:

Husband, Bobby, for his patience and understanding
Family and friends for their support and encouragement
Shoestring Software for dealing with my computer gremlins
Linda Acaster, my mentor at the Open College of the Arts, for inspiring this collection
Lyn Webster Wilde, my Hereford course tutor, for prompting my foray into dreaming
My friends at the Friday Writers Group for their constructive advice
Hugh Morris for his expertise with the camera
Butford Publishing for making this book possible

Destiny's Footprints – Literary Credentials

The Scavenger – first published by Biscuit Publishing in *The Sensitively Thin Bill of the Shag*

The Happy Season – to be published in anthology

Dream On – highly commended by *Writers' Forum* magazine

Hearth to Hearth – highly commended by *Writers' Forum* magazine

Boxes – first published in *Scribble* magazine

Loving Spirit – to be published in anthology

Missing Data – highly commended in *Viewpoint* competition; first published in *The Lady* magazine

Child of Destiny – shortlisted in *Countryside Tales* competition and runner-up for *Legend Writing Award*

Feet First – commended in *Viewpoint* competition

Cake Comfort – first published in *Senior Moments* magazine

Quietus – highly commended by *Writers' Forum* magazine

release dot com – shortlisted in *Viewpoint* competition; shortlisted by *Writers' Forum* magazine

A Raw Talent – highly commended by *Writers' Forum* magazine; award winner in *Francis Brett Young* competition

Over the Rainbow – Certificate of Merit in Mere Literary Festival

Don't Go Back – first published in *Writers' Forum* magazine

Preface

Short stories are an exciting challenge, trying to catch the reader's imagination with a character whose life is changed in some way in so few words. They are but a glimpse into another's world, provoking thought and emotion.

I have always loved the short story, reading a variety of magazines, popular and small press, to which I eventually contributed. As life progressed, so my markets expanded and, although time was sometimes scarce, the short story form continued to fascinate. With a folder bulging at the seams I sought publication for a collection. Here it is – *Destiny's Footprints*.

I chose this title because, in each story, the main character takes a step forward on their natural or chosen destiny in life. The themes are varied, from humorous to murderous, a gentle slice of life to the supernatural.

I hope the stories give you as much pleasure reading them as they gave me in their creation.

I dreamed my life was but a dream,
myself just pure perception,
and spirits came and lifted me
beyond my stark identity.

Lightened, I floated high
and spun beyond reality,
where all on earth became a speck
of dust, a mirage of mortality.

The Scavenger

The first sign of fear came from the birds. Crows circled, cawing, screaming, spiralling upwards. Starlings followed, shrieking, one dark mass soaring into the thin grey clouds that had suddenly hidden the spring sun. Aislie stood in the meadow, watching the heaving wings disappear into infinity and wondered what had spooked them. No human being was visible on the farm, the meadows stretching greenly behind her to the farmhouse, a smudged pencil sketch in the distance.

She shivered. The warmth had beckoned her, torn her from her painting, and she had breathed the fresh sweet smell of hedgerows budding, primroses and dewy grass.

Father was ploughing the first turn of the year and mother busied herself baking, a domestic scene that had framed her childhood, but fettered her now as she longed to escape the solitude of the soft hills, a longing poured into her paintings, paintings of tall buildings, moonswept roofs, neon lights brightly daubed and rows of people, people in the streets at night, people living in the nights; her dreams fed these scenes.

She would go there, one day, it was a promise, a promise whispered in dark nights as the wind howled and snow lashed the peaks, a whisper seeping through the cold windows and slipping into obscurity. Each summer when father traipsed the hedgerows, blocking escape routes for the lambs, she saw her dream of freedom bondaged too.

Her thoughts were whirled away with the birds as their cries lessened and fragmented, faint screams silencing and then nothing moved, no birdsong piped, and through the grey mist she saw a darker shadow, gliding nearer, grey, yellow-grey, yellow suited and hooded, arms and legs spread-eagled, swaying, swooping to the ground. It was a man, lying inert, flat on his stomach in the meadow.

She stepped nearer as he slowly coiled and sat up. The hood fell from his face and dark curls cascaded to his shoulders. His eyes met hers, green-blue eyes, eyes the colour of the swimming pool, in the shallow end. They showed no surprise at her presence.

"Shouldn't you have a parachute?" She wondered why he wasn't hurt.

He smiled. "Have you never heard of free-falling?"

"What, all the way down?"

"It's not widely advertised, too dangerous, but yes, it's possible."

"So I see."

She felt no fear of the stranger and, as he stood up and freed himself from his suit, she saw he was quite normal in appearance. Older than herself maybe, but sure in his movements, at ease with his circumstances. He folded the suit amazingly small and tucked it into his bag. He stood looking at her, his pale eyes assessing, a faint frown on his brow.

"Well, Aislie," his voice was amused, gentle, "will you come with me?"

He held out his hand and, unthinking, she took it. Walking beside him across the meadow, the farm and its fetters fell away and her mind opened to the future.

"You fell badly," Meridon said, watching her as he sat on the bed.

Aislie frowned, her fingers following the line of bandage around her forehead. She remembered the sudden panic, the ground swaying in her vision, her relaxed arms tensing and her fingers reaching forward. Then her swooping descent degenerating into a hellish plummet, the ground relentlessly hard, and she was rolling, hurting and then the searing crunch to her head, shards of lightening in her brain, pain and blessed darkness; until now. She looked around the room. The light was strong, too harsh for her eyes. She winced.

"Where am I?"

"You're at home." Meridon leaned forward and brushed her brow.

Aislie stared at the stranger. "Who are you?"

"Meridon. You don't remember?" She shook her head, fear lurching in her stomach. "We went skydiving, you needed inspiration for your painting. You were lost, ideas had stagnated; we went free-falling."

Aislie leaned back on the pillows, defeated.

"Rest," Meridon ordered. "I'll be back later."

He left the room and Aislie succumbed to the numbness. She was afraid. Dark tendrils of thought drifted into her consciousness. She remembered the birds; great swooping shadows in her mind, wings disturbing, calls shuddering through her being. The birds, she felt the shaking begin again. Meridon must be right, they were skydiving. How else would she have seen the birds?

She couldn't remember. The room was unfamiliar – would she really have chosen such sombre-coloured drapes? And Meridon, did she love him? He had said 'home' and she occupied a double bed; so she lived with him? For some reason the thought terrified her, jarred her reasoning, evoked the same sickening fear that she recalled as she fell, fell through the birds. 'Meridon', she tried the syllables over her tongue, 'Meridon', but the name was clumsy to her. What had he said about painting? She needed inspiration? Painting, brushes on canvas, that was a comforting muse, familiar? Maybe. The effort of focusing her senses throbbed through her head and she relinquished her brain to the shadows. She let the dreams overcome reality and slipped into darkness.

'*Paintings by Aislie*' – the banner filled her with pride. Her own exhibition, and in a prominent part of town. Twelve months hard work accumulating in this, and she couldn't have done it without the help of Meridon.

She still wasn't sure exactly how she had met Meridon or from whence she had come to his home. Her memories of her horrendous fall remained confused, but she had ceased to question his answers. All that mattered was her painting. She stood in front of the largest, a spring scene in the country, details taken from vague memories that haunted the grey areas of her mind. She knew it was good. Did it exist, this place immortalised with her brushes? She didn't know and it was no longer important.

"Can't you remember?" Meridon persisted. She shook her head.

She had asked herself the same question when her brushes had created her first picture. A farmhouse, surrounded by fields, green blossoming hedges, a figure beneath the roses, faint, shadowy.

"I remember nothing. You explained my past, before the fall; how we met here in the city and went skydiving. You hadn't known me long. You can't answer my pleas for knowledge of my childhood; it must have been here in the city, there is nowhere else, no one has claimed me despite my search. Perhaps I have no family. I have to believe you, I have no other truth."

Meridon appeared satisfied with her replies. She loved her studio, alien though it appeared at first. Her paintings were successful and made them a good income; she was somehow surprised by this. Meridon was her agent, he informed her, as well as her lover. She accepted this information and concentrated on her painting.

Colours spewed, animals stirred, wind-lashed trees bowed and the air flowed, incandescent through the shifting hedgerows. Her imagination conjured delicate buds, sprayed shafts of ethereal flowers; her heart was overwhelmed with an abundance of joy and she purged it all onto canvas. Her paintings left her exhausted as if her soul had been wrung through her fingertips and splurged for exploitation.

Her exhibition was a success. She wandered quietly behind the viewers, listening to their comments.

"They're so realistic!" The man was studying the farmyard scene, animals feeding, fields forming a backcloth. "You'd think she'd actually seen a farm. She certainly has imagination."

"The history books are pretty good on description. After all, farming was a way of life decades ago; unimaginable to me, but there you are, it was an interesting era."

"Fascinating," agreed his companion. "It must have been a strange existence."

"That's what all modern generations think about the past. It's difficult to imagine a world other than the one we live in."

"Yes, but all that empty land, animals roaming around, barbaric!"

Her paintings decorated Meridon's great house; there were none like it, until she found the watercolour in the summerhouse. She had wandered in the sunshine through the walled garden that dimmed the traffic noise and offered peace. Spring flowers bloomed in disarray, carefully nurtured in the malodorous air. In the far corner a summerhouse nestled and she pushed the long grasses aside and crept into the dusty gloom. A grimy table, a forgotten chair, and the picture.

She wiped the debris from the glass and the colours thrust themselves into the light. Carefully she carried the frame outside and studied the scene. A river, silver in the sunshine, grassy banks and birds. It was the birds that caught a fragment in her mind. She hadn't seen birds since her fall and there they were, beautifully caught in wing-fluttering movement. She carried her find to the house. She wasn't sure why she was nervous, but her stomach churned with familiar fear as she studied the birds. The dark shadows that hunched on the edges of her mind spewed wafts of terror that flicked through her blood. She set the canvas on an easel and awaited Meridon's return.

"Who painted this?"

Meridon stared at the picture; his body so still she felt the tautness of his perception touch her exposed doubts. His eyes, when they travelled slowly to her face, pierced her senses with shards of menace. She drew a shuddering breath and looked away.

"Aislie." His voice was soft and she looked again at his face. The smile was warm, his eyes gentle and she wondered if her disturbed senses had been mistaken. "That was painted by a protégé of mine, a long while ago." He took the painting and balanced it against the wall. "She was successful, for a while, then she lost interest; and so, of course, did I. I cannot be an agent to a failure." His eyes devoured the brush strokes. "Where did you find this?"

"In the summerhouse." Her voice trembled slightly.

"Ah!" He let out a deep breath. "I had forgotten..." He seemed lost in thought.

"Where is she now?"

He shrugged and cast the painting aside, casually, as if of no importance. "Not here." He took her arm. "Come, we have your paintings to package, ready for collection. We will have to arrange another exhibition, when you have filled the studio again."

She allowed herself to be led away and when she returned later the painting had gone. She was uneasy but afraid to mention it again and, for the next few weeks, she concentrated on her new collection.

She wasn't sure when the memories began to dim. Gradually, they faded beyond recognition. She found herself painting buildings, streets, people masses. Meridon was annoyed.

"These won't sell, Aislie. There are hundreds of artists painting the world of cities. Yours are famous for their difference."

She searched her mind for detail but the sombre mantle that eclipsed her vision spread insidiously through her brain. Birds, she could visualise birds, great funereal atrocities sweeping their wings through her consciousness, and she splattered them in horrific lesions across the canvas. She would tear the pitiless offerings to shreds as Meridon watched, his eyes carefully veiled, but his quiescence spawned familiar dread in her soul.

"Remember," he would insinuate softly in her ear as they shared the consuming bed, "remember, Aislie, look back in your dreams."

And she'd drift into slumber, pushing her mind open to positive visions, and pray as she slipped beyond reality, beyond the city streets to the celestial night that had once cosseted a farm in the country. It was useless. She studied previous paintings but her mind remained a blank. She became despondent.

"You need a break." Meridon's voice was gentle. "We'll go

skydiving, free-fall, your mind will refresh in the air. Remember the last time, the inspiration that followed, the exhibition."

Aislie felt terror twist her stomach. "I could be hurt again!"

"Not this time." His voice was gently compelling. "This time you won't look down, this time you'll float your arms, it will be all right, trust me."

'Trust me.' The words seared Aislie's mind with foreboding. He propelled her forward and, shaking, Aislie followed him into the plane. They wheeled above the clouds. Meridon took her hand and together they plummeted from the plane, arms and legs spread-eagled. He smiled and let go of her clutching fingers. Very gently he wheeled away from her vision, merging into a thin grey cloud that blocked the sun. She called his name but the wind tore the words to shreds of cloud and her heart was filled with fear. She heard birds call and saw crows and starlings circling her descent, shrieking, screaming. They swooped about her, their wind tunnels rocking her movements and then she hit the ground.

It took a few minutes to regain her breath and then she brushed the hair from her face and sat up. The grass was still damp from the early dew and she brushed droplets from her arms. Her head hurt and she felt the warm stickiness of blood on her temple. She had bounced over a tuft of grass, landed against a stone. She spat on a tissue and stemmed the trickle that slid slimily towards her ear. It was only a scratch but she ached and her head throbbed. The grey clouds parted and the early morning sun blazed gaily over the farm. She turned and limped back to the farmhouse.

"Your breakfast's nearly spoilt," her mother grumbled and placed the plate of bacon and eggs in front of Aislie.

"I'm famished." She attacked the plate with gusto, a smile on her face. "It's going to be a beautiful day."

Her father grunted as he came through the door. "Five more lambs," he commented in satisfaction. "Healthy too. Have to watch the crows though, circling the field they are, scavenging for the frail ones."

Aislie left the kitchen and went into the small dining room she used as a studio. She stared at the painting on her easel. Buildings, streets, masses of people. She shuddered and, reaching for the canvas, tore it into thin shreds. Why on earth had she painted such grimness? Her head still ached from her fall and she stared at the blank canvas, her brush poised. She began to paint, dipping her brush and casting bold swathes of black across the skyline.

'Birds,' she thought, 'great crows and starlings, circling.' Her brush followed her memories and swept swiftly. 'Birds, and lambs, poor weak lambs, waiting to be scavenged.'

It was bold, it was good and she felt triumphant and yet, as she watched the carnage develop, she shuddered and her disturbed mind allowed the shadows to permeate her vision as she splashed a final drop of bright red blood.

She was exhausted, her horror exorcised, and she turned the painting to the wall. She filled her mind with the farm at sunrise, dew glistening on the grass, newborn lambs tottering over the tufts and she started a new canvas, a golden glow suffusing the skyline.

"That's more like it." She sighed. Wearily she put her brushes to soak and let lethargy propel her from the room.

In the kitchen her mother had just put down the phone. "That was Jane Morgan, she says the Council have put an order on their farm. They've got to sell."

Her father frowned. "Government expansion plans! If they have their way they'll build all over the good land. There are too many people to house, not enough room in the cities anymore. Ridiculous I call it. How can we breed animals for food if they take our land? Folks have got to eat."

"It's all this new thinking," her mother moaned. "Vegetarian. No need for meat soon, no need for animals. It's a sad state of affairs." She sighed heavily and opened the oven door, putting the joint of beef to roast.

Her father snorted in disgust. "Soon there'll be no farms left. Then what will folks do? The countryside will be history!"

The Happy Season

The shed doors were flung wide, open to the sun, the smell of freshly picked raspberries wafting from the loaded tables as I stood, dwarfed in a shadow, and stared at her.

She was about my age, but she looked clean and fresh. Her fair hair shone in the sunbeams and her delicate fingers tipped and weighed the fruit into punnets ready for market.

"What d'yer want?" The man's voice was sharp, his lips a thin gash in bristle-padded cheeks.

I started in fright. In my awe I had been unaware of his bulk emerging from the far corner. 'Hoity-toity,' Mam called him, this man who fetched us in the rattling old van to pick the fruit.

"Thinks he's better 'an us," she'd grumbled to Gran last night as she stirred the stew.

"Just because he drives us about, seems to forget he was born two doors down. Now in a farm cottage, would you believe. Don't make him no better."

She'd grimaced darkly and cut the bread for morning. "Such a nice lad, he used to be."

Gran glanced shrewdly at her. "Should have gone to war, same as the rest. Might have done him some good."

"His back was bad." Mam cut savagely at a piece of cheese.

"Huh!" Gran snorted and her knitting needles clacked. "Twenty years old and a bad back! Wan't so bad he couldn't get young Daisy in the club, and her just out of school."

"He married her and got a job," Mam protested.

"Should think so too, poor mite. Heard she's having another. That makes four. And her no more than skin and bone herself."

Gran sighed and her needles clicked furiously. When Gran was angry she could knit a whole pair of socks in an evening.

Mam had a far away look in her eyes as she emptied the teapot in the sink. "He was a useful lad," she said.

"Useful!" Gran muttered.

"He helped us all, while the menfolk were fighting."

"Aye. He helped you women too much I'm thinking."

Mam reached for the kettle. "Tea?" she asked quickly, and I noticed her cheeks had flushed.

"Molly should be in bed." Gran eyed me suddenly. "She'll be too tired for the picking tomorrow else."

I slunk reluctantly upstairs. I was excited about tomorrow. I'd never been allowed to go fruit picking before.

It would be dark when the van called, sneaking through the council houses, picking up yawning women and whining kids. Sometimes the menfolk went along, if they weren't working, and often as not they weren't. Not many had found work after the war. No amount of promises had made the world a better place, for all the fighting.

Dad never went.

"I ain't fruit picking," he'd bellow when Mam snapped that a couple of days in the fresh air would do him good.

"Women's work! Old Joe needs a hand with his building. I promised."

The trouble was, Joe could never pay Dad and the rent man would be knocking on the door for what we owed again soon. He'd got nasty last time and the social wouldn't help. Said they'd given Dad the money. When Mam asked him for it, he cursed her. In the nick of time, it seemed, the fruit picking started.

As a small child it had felt a magical time. Gran minded me at home, cradling me on her knee and telling me I was precious. A precious hope, she called me, born to celebrate Dad's coming home from the war.

She'd tell me other stories too, stories about princesses and handsome princes. It was a good time. She'd rock me to sleep and her voice would crackle softly as she sang '*Bye Baby Bunting*' over and over. In the season I'd feel warm and wanted. Even Mam seemed happy and the rent man patted me on the head when he called. A magical time!

The next morning I stumbled sleepily from the house. As the women climbed into the van they exchanged backchat with the driver.

"Don't you be cheeky with *me*. Don't forget I'm drivin'." He laughed and I stared at his bulky frame, hypnotised. He was a fearsome man.

His rough hand rubbed my cheek as I passed and I winced as a sharp fingernail caught my skin.

"Teaching this 'un young, eh, Maggie?"

"She'm old enough," Mam retorted and pushed me into the cold, dark bowels of the van.

"I don't doubt it, if she'm anything like her mam!"

Mam shoved me angrily.

The old van was full of wooden boxes and the women perched on them, hunched together as we rocked over the uneven road. Sometimes they toppled from their unstable seats and crushed us children huddled on the floor. Then they cursed and swore until the laughter in the driver's seat stopped and abuse echoed over our heads.

It seemed a long way and, as the back doors were opened, I blinked as the sun's early rays blinded me and we spilled onto the grass. I was petrified as I stared at the fields and hedges, stretching as far as I could see. Not a house in sight. I had never felt so small and afraid.

"Now don't you get wandering off," Mam warned me. "You could get lost round here easy. Just you stay with me."

I needed no further bidding and scuttled behind her to the great rows of raspberry canes stretching over the hill.

"Now then…" She handed me a basket. "You pick the ones down here and stick with me, do you hear?"

I nodded.

Mam's fingers were nimble. Her baskets filled quickly. I tried my best but I was used to holding firm to anything I caught and took a while to learn not to squash the berries. Juice stained my pinny and dripped through my fingers but I soon got the hang of it.

"Take those baskets to the shed and get 'em weighed. They book 'em in."

"By myself?"

"Course by yourself. Make yourself useful. Follow the row down. The shed's at the bottom. Then come straight back."

It seemed a long way down the row. The uneven soil beneath my feet almost caused me to trip, but I carried the baskets carefully, fearful lest I should spill any of the precious fruit.

By the time I reached the shed I was panting, the baskets feeling as heavy as Mam's coal bucket. The shed was enormous, as big as our Church Hall and twice as daunting. I stood in the doorway and it was then I saw her.

She smiled shyly at me, glancing sideways at the man who humped the boxes and shifted the laden baskets. I thought she looked like the princess in the book Gran had bought me from the Jumble Sale last Christmas.

I looked down at my thin frock, the pattern almost faded away and was conscious of my dirty toe peeping through my shoe. I should have washed. My pinny was stained and Mam had forgotten to take a brush to my hair that morning.

"Hello." Her voice was gentle, friendly.

I stared at her, still clutching my baskets.

"Give 'em here." The man had come to me and reached for the handles.

My fingers curled tightly.

"Mam says you'm to weigh 'em and book 'em." I glared at him.

"Course!" He laughed, his eyes sweeping me boldly. I shivered. The tin handles scratched my palms as he pulled them away and I saw him place them on the platform and weight the scales till they balanced. He scribbled in a red book.

"All done." He grinned at me and I backed away. He made me fearful.

"Tell your Mam I wouldn't dare cheat on her!"

"I'm Rosalind. What's your name?" The girl had left the table and was by my side.

"Molly." I stared at her.

"Do you want to come and play?"

I gaped. "Where?"

"They're making hay in the next field. It's fun."

"I'll have to ask Mam."

She shrugged and turned back to the fruit. "Go and ask. I'll wait."

The man ruffled her hair, gently this time. "Poor little 'un. Lonely eh? I'll come and play with you."

She looked at him in a way I'd seen our preacher look, when one of the boys played tricks in Church, but he just laughed and turned away, heaving three boxes together into the back of the van.

I scurried back to the field.

"Can I, Mam, can I go and play?"

"You'm here to pick fruit, we needs the money. Can't afford to be playing."

I sighed. It was the answer I'd expected.

It seemed a long morning and then the sound of a tractor made Mam raise her head, grin and put down the basket.

"Time for food."

Thankfully I followed her down the row and sank onto the grass beneath the hedge.

I heard Rosalind's voice, laughing. She was walking by a tall man who laughed back at her, his jolly face smiling at us. I heard her call him 'Dad' and I stared up at him nervously.

"Well, my dears? It's good to see you again. You've all survived the winter?"

He laughed again and Mam smiled from a rosy face as she took the tin can from his hands.

"Tea is it, and nothing stronger?"

"Tea, my dear, hot and sweet, nothing stronger till the end of season. I want the fruit picked afore the rain comes."

"Won't come for weeks!" shouted someone.

"Wouldn't dare!" came a reply, and they all laughed and settled to their food and tea.

Rosalind smiled at me and then clutched her father's sleeve as he marched back to his tractor and set off for the next field. Rosalind stood on the drawbar, wedged between his seat and the wheel fender as he churned his way through the ruts.

Then it was back to picking. Just when my fingers began to turn numb Mam relented.

"You've done well today, Molly. Go and play a while. It'll soon be time to go home. But stay close and listen for the van when he blows the horn. He won't wait."

Eagerly I ran down the row and halted in a rush of breath at the shed door.

"Come on." Rosalind caught my hand and we ran across the tufted grass towards a gate. Lithely she climbed over. I followed, falling the last two rungs and grazing my leg. Blood trickled slowly into my shoe but I was too excited to notice.

The cut grass scratched my ankles as Rosalind led the way to a stack of bales. I'd never seen the like!

"There's my house." Rosalind pointed to a tiled roof peeking through the trees and I gazed at her. It did indeed look like the fairy castle in my book.

"Where's your Mam?"

"Mum's at home. She'll be here in the fields just now. She always comes to do the final weighing and to pay everyone. Dad just organises."

"I'd best be getting back." I slid down the bales scratching arms and legs.

"You'll come again?" I heard her call, and I nodded as I scrambled over the gate.

Mam hardly glanced at me as I clutched her apron and reached for a basket. My fingers trembled as I stretched between the spiked canes for the raspberries. I hummed '*Bye Baby Bunting*' and thought of Gran.

I fell asleep in the van on the way home. The floor was hard and dirty but I was beyond care.

Mam was smiling and the sandwich tins were full of fruit. There would be pies in the oven and jam for our bread. Silver coins clinked in pockets and the rent man didn't seem quite so fearsome.

Tired voices cracked jokes and the sun set in a red sky. A good omen for the morning. It was the start of the season and I was part of it.

Dream On

"I always knew I was destined to meet the spirits of the dead," Alysha told Philip on their first date.

Philip speared a piece of cucumber from the Greek salad that was piled between them. "And have you? Communicated with the spirits?" He kept his voice light.

"Not yet." Alysha scooped a piece of feta cheese and soaked her bread in the herb-scented oil. "I've felt...," she hesitated, "shadowed presences. But I will meet them, when I'm ready."

"I see."

Philip had finally plucked up courage to ask Alysha for a meal after their third evening class. She was beautiful, with ebony hair and large, smoky eyes dominating her delicate features.

They were both studying Greek. She, because she was fascinated with the mythology and felt there was more chance of meeting ghosts amongst those ancient stones than anywhere else; he, because he loved the islands. As a budding lawyer, he liked to feel in control and therefore, if he intended to travel regularly to Greece, he needed to know the language.

She smiled now at his startled expression, a smile so sweet it somersaulted his heart and caused a flutter in his fingers. Her investigative look made him feel inadequate, a feeling so alien it was painful. With his fair curls and eyes the colour of forget-me-nots he was used to admiration. Alysha was different. He flashed her his disarming smile, but the corners of his mouth trembled slightly.

"You think I'm nuts?" She laughed.

He shook his head. "Let's just say I've an open mind," he replied, which was totally untrue.

She studied him for a moment, and then touched his hand lightly across the table. "I think it's time for the moussaka?"

The Greek lessons finished in April. By then Philip was in love with Alysha and felt no hesitation in agreeing to a holiday on the Greek island of Skopelos.

"A whole week of sun, sea and sand!" He grinned at her as they dined in their favourite restaurant.

"No sand," Alysha corrected, smiling. "But beaches and beautiful fish-filled sea." She studied him for a moment. "And an exciting archaeological find," she added quietly.

Philip grimaced. "I suppose we have to do some exploring?"

"Of course," Alysha said lightly. "But only for a few hours. We'll swim and laze, and eat!" She grinned. "You can stay on the beach while I visit the historical sites, if you want."

Philip sighed. "I expect I'll manage a few hours of exercise, it will do me good."

The journey was tedious, but, finally, the ferry from Skiathos rounded the bay and Skopelos spread before them. Orange-roofed houses snuggled in pine-covered mountains, the white walls sparkling in the evening sun. Skopelos town itself was splayed around the harbour, tavernas spilling onto the water's edge and, as they disembarked, a feeling of peace surrounded the tired pair.

Hugging Alysha close, Philip opened the apartment door and, ignoring their luggage, they snuggled gratefully into the soft bed. They slept the clock round, waking to the calls of fishermen on the quay, selling the harvest of their night fishing.

For two days they meandered through narrow streets, holding hands and laughing, their joy in each other exuberant. They swam from glorious beaches and dined in tavernas to the sound of Greek melodies and the plash of the ghostly boats on the glittering water; until Alysha suggested a visit inland. Philip studied the hired Fiat doubtfully, but Alysha drove it gently up the winding track that led through scattered villages, the islanders on their donkeys showing but a passing interest.

They passed through Glysteri and followed the signpost for Karia.

"Where are we going?" Philip was curious as he stared up at the towering heights of Mount Delphi.

"You'll see!" Alysha was wriggling with suppressed excitement.

She parked the car in a clearing and they set off on foot. A meandering goat path led upwards through scattered rocks and miniature cyclamen. The pungent smell of wild sage mingled with the scent of pines and, as they climbed, silence enfolded them.

Great mounds of boulders surrounded circular grassed areas and Philip stopped, breathing heavily.

"What is this place?" He reached for his bottle of water and sat on a ledge.

Alysha's eyes were sparkling. "There was an earthquake here, in recent years, and the quake shifted the rocks. On the summit are the Sendoukia graves."

"The what?"

"Ancient tombs, cut by hand into the rock. The quake moved the boulders that covered them."

"I see." Reluctantly, Philip got to his feet and followed Alysha, who was bounding ahead.

Even Philip had to admit the tombs were awe-inspiring, although he couldn't repress a shudder as he gazed into their depths. Carved deep, the sides were polished smooth, and his imagination conjured a head resting on the hewn stone pillows. Taking a deep breath he turned away and stared at the great wedges of rock that had been guarding the tombs.

"Wow!" He coughed to revive his voice. "How on earth did they manage to close them?"

Alysha shrugged. "Ancient peoples were amazing. Their strength must have been terrific." She was staring down into the graves. "Just imagine…"

"I'd rather not!" Philip turned his gaze to the panorama of

islands that spread before him. They were alone on the silent mountain and Philip shivered. If ever Alysha was going to meet her spirits, it was easy to imagine it could be in this place. He put an arm across her shoulders, feeling her bare skin beneath his fingers, and pulled her close. She was reassuringly warm and he kissed the softness of her hair.

"There must have been a settlement here." Alysha was gazing around her. "Maybe cave houses, or stone buildings against the mountain. I wish... I want to explore a little?" She turned her dark eyes beseechingly to Philip and he smiled, loosening his hold.

"Of course. I didn't expect you to go straight back down!" He settled on a smooth boulder. "I've brought my book and a picnic. I'll wait here until you've done your communicating!"

Alysha gave a wry smile. "Don't mock me!"

"I'm not!" Philip grinned. "Want a sandwich?"

Alysha shook her head and wandered round Sendoukia. Philip opened his novel and gave a sigh of satisfaction as he bit into feta cheese. He was quite happy now and the walk back down would be easier. And then, perhaps, they'd have a couple of hours on the beach. Yes, he was enjoying this holiday.

Alysha climbed over the rocks, exploring deeper into the mountain. The air was very still and she could feel the hairs on her skin rising in expectation. She rounded a cracked cliff face and caught her breath. There, in front of her, was a fissure in the mountain, wide enough for a person to enter. She squeezed through the narrow aperture and stood still. It felt very cold and she heard the drip of water. As her eyes grew accustomed to the gloom she saw the tunnel widened slightly and yes, she could see a shimmer of radiance in the distance.

Moving slowly, her feet slipping on the shingle, she felt her way forwards. The walls were slimy and the atmosphere pungent, smelling of damp earth and pine roots.

Her senses sharpened and she felt excitement creep through her bones. Where was this place? Had anyone been here before her?

The glow increased and seemed to sparkle, bouncing off the walls and making her shade her eyes. Suddenly, the tunnel opened onto a ledge. Below her, steps led downwards and, as she paused at the head of the stairway, her eyes took in the scene before her. She felt the hackles rise on the base of her neck and felt the thrum of the atmosphere as it weaved around her head and insinuated into her brain. For the first time, she felt a ripple of fear skirt the edges of her mind.

Philip reached the end of his novel and closed the book with a sigh of pleasure. That had been good, brilliantly written and totally enthralling. So enthralling he hadn't checked the time once and he gave a start now as he realised he had been alone for over two hours.

Oh my God! He sprang to his feet. What if she had fallen on the loose rock? Fallen down the mountainside and was even now lying injured, or even unconscious? His heart thundered against his ribs and fear cracked his voice as he called her name.

"Alysha, Alysha!"

The sound invaded the trembling silence and shocked him.

"Calm down," he muttered. "Think!" She'd got her mobile phone with her. He checked his for any sign of a message but his was dumbly blank.

"Damn!"

What on earth should he do now? It was miles back to the car, and he wasn't sure where to go for help. Night would fall soon and he didn't fancy being alone in the dark in this God-forsaken place!

At that moment, as his fear turned to panic, he heard a skittering of shale. Gulping, he turned. Alysha stood there, staring at him.

"Alysha! Thank God!" Philip stumbled towards her and wrapped his arms around her, hugging her close. She felt stone-cold.

"Where have you been?" He held her at arms length and studied her face. "I was so worried."

"Exploring." Her voice was cool and her eyes distant. "I was exploring, Philip, I told you."

She looked across the mountain at the deepening azure of the sea. "Shall we go?"

Without waiting for an answer she turned and set off down the track. Philip grabbed his rucksack, stuffing his book and bags into it. He didn't want to lose sight of her again.

"Wait, Alysha, wait for me."

She paused and, looking over her shoulder, smiled at him. "I'm waiting, Philip," she said quietly. "Don't panic!"

"So…" They had descended in silence, Philip still anxious. "So, Alysha, did you find anything exciting?"

She opened the car door and then stood very still, staring back up the mountain. "What did you think I might find?" She smiled at him as she slid into the passenger seat and Philip was relieved to see she seemed normal again.

"Oh…" He started the engine. "I don't know." He kept his voice light. "Maybe a few spirits?" And he laughed.

"I see." Alysha smiled a secret smile and glanced back over her shoulder. As they rounded the corner, the mountain receded.

"Well?" He glanced at her and she tucked a hand under his arm.

"Let's eat in tonight. I feel like an early night." She leaned against him as he manoeuvred the gear stick with difficulty.

"Wonderful idea!" He grinned happily; hardly realising she hadn't answered his question.

The next day Philip suggested a day on the beach. Alysha had been withdrawn the previous evening and, although she agreed with a smile, Philip couldn't help but feel that her thoughts were elsewhere.

"Let's laze." He slipped an arm around her waist and kissed her cheek. "Swim and eat and laze. I want a suntan to go home with."

She packed her bag and he sought out a picnic. Adding a bottle of wine, he humped his rucksack onto his shoulder and they set off for the beach. Finding a secluded corner between rocks, he spread out his towel and gave a sigh of pleasure.

"Now, this is what I call a holiday!"

Alysha was sitting, staring out to sea.

"Alysha?" He rubbed her shoulder and she gave a deep sigh of anguish. "What's the matter?"

"I have to go back," she said, her voice trembling. "Now."

"Back?" He stared at her. "Back where?"

"To Sendoukia." She stood up.

"Now?"

"Now." She nodded. "You stay here. I shan't be long. I'll see you at the apartment later."

And, before he could protest, she had gone, striding purposefully across the beach.

Sighing, he lay back and squinted at the sun. What on earth was the matter with her? And whatever should he do? Nothing, he supposed. She obviously wanted to go alone. But, as he stared moodily at the brilliant sky, he felt utterly miserable.

Bounding to his feet, he ran over the shingle and plunged into the icy water. Gasping, he struck out and vent his annoyance in a strong crawl that inched him away from the shore, until, his arms aching, he turned over and floated lazily, drifting slowly back with the tide.

The next day he was ready for her. "I'm coming with you," he said in a determined voice. "I'm not spending another day on my own." He glared at Alysha.

It had been almost dark when Alysha had returned the previous evening and then she had lain down and gone to sleep. He'd been angry, and bewildered.

"OK." She shrugged. "Come and see."

The journey to Sendoukia was silent and he followed her up the familiar path, a frown on his brow. He hesitated at the fissure but, as Alysha quickly disappeared from sight, he followed.

Fear engulfed him as he stumbled through the tunnel until, at last, he ventured onto the ledge, and caught his breath. Slowly the shifting amber fog parted as he shaded his eyes. Incandescent towers pierced the luminous cloud, radiant sunshine reflecting from their shimmering heights. Spires, domes were unveiling before his startled eyes, delicate buildings seeming hewn from the golden rock, glittering as rays caught their curves. He looked up. There was no sunshine, just the inky blackness of the cave roof.

His heart thudded as he reverted his gaze to the town below. Along the marbled streets small figures wafted, smiling, an aura of serenity surrounding each. They spoke, although the air was silent, and he felt himself drawn to the pure beauty and peace of the scene. Who were these people?

He turned to Alysha, slowly, lest his movement caused the image to disappear.

"What do you see?" she whispered to Philip.

"I see waif-like people, dressed in flowing white, floating through a city with sparkling spires; such joy, and peace," he said in a hoarse voice.

He felt Alysha sigh at his side.

"What do you see?" He turned to her.

"Nothing."

"Nothing?" His heart jumped in terror. "Nothing?" He was shouting.

"Ssh!" She pulled his sleeve. "Come away."

The sunlight was welcome and he suddenly realised he was shivering, his fingers white with cold. They sat on a rock and gazed at the distance-hazed islands.

"What did you mean, nothing?" he ventured at last.

She turned and looked at him, her eyes calm. "I saw spirits, and spirits are nothing."

He felt uneasy as she continued.

"The cave was full of warm, enveloping, golden light; no shapes, just millions of amber motes dancing and wafting together."

"But I saw people," he insisted.

"You don't believe in spirits. Your conscious mind will only accept images that are logical, so it converts the spirits into a logical image – people."

"Now wait a minute…"

"I believe in the essence of life, phantoms that inhabit our bodies, souls if you like. They live with us for a lifetime, then return to their universe."

"Which is?"

"Eternity. Have you ever thought that life is but a dream?"

He stared at her for a moment. "Have you ever thought of seeing a psychiatrist?"

She grinned. "Frequently! But seriously, how do you know we're not dreaming, that we are *real*. Mightn't everything be a hallucination of our subconscious mind? The spirit has to abide somewhere, as mine abides in my body."

"And that looks real enough to me!" He stood up and caught her hand. "Come on, let's get back to the beach. All this is making me very uncomfortable and, whether I'm a figment of my imagination or not, this figment is decidedly hungry!"

She followed him down the mountain and, with a last look at the shadowed heights, allowed him to drive her away.

Lying on the beach, the images faded in Philip's mind. Had it all been a dream? Had his imagination been beguiled, seduced by Alysha's fantasies?

"Was there really anything there?" he asked, propping himself on his elbow and staring into her serene face.

"Of course." She smiled. "I told you, the spirits were meeting there. Yesterday, I mingled with them."

"Am I supposed to believe that?"

She shrugged. "Please yourself. You have to realise the soul of your being can be anywhere." She sat up, a serious look on her face. "Our bodies are but images that our brain can accept. The spirit is extrinsic, ethereal, beyond description."

She lay back down as she saw his sceptical expression. "I don't want to discuss it any more."

They spent their last day wandering the sloping streets of Skopelos and buying trinkets. Alysha didn't mention the subject again and Philip was relieved, convincing himself the ambience and the wine had incited a hallucination. He wondered if their romance could withstand Alysha's preoccupation with the supernatural and hoped that, once they returned to England, life would become normal again. He felt pleased to be packing, and disappointed.

The ferry crossing was swift and silent. In the airport they drank coffee from plastic cups, their conversation desultory. At last, the plane rumbled down the runway and, with a shuddering lurch, left Skiathos. Alysha had her eyes closed. Philip reached over and took her hand in his. It was icy cold.

A tourist, panting his way towards the top of the trail to Sendoukia, caught a glimmer of stardust from the corner of his eye. Turning sharply, his gaze searched the pines that swayed in the breeze and he shook his head, perplexed. He strained his ears as the sound of hushed whispers wafted on the wind and his eyes scanned the shadowed summit.

A feeling of disquiet trembled across his mind. He rubbed his hands, surprised at their coldness and, shrugging uneasily, turned and retraced his steps to the waiting hire car.

Hearth to Hearth

The day the Fun Club was formed Tom Parker was banished from his chair in the Snug at The Jolly Duck and relegated to a barstool. He was furious.

Every evening, since moving to his retirement cottage in the village, he had ensconced himself in the Snug on the horsehair chair in front of the blazing log fire, feet on the hearth, and contemplated his life. It was cosy in the Snug. The company was congenial and the occasional raucous laughter from the bar enlivened the evenings. He was content.

From the safety of the Snug he could now acknowledge that his life had been hard, but fruitful. A good career in banking, a loyal wife who, if her tongue was sharp, had structured his life until her passing, God rest her soul, and left him with the means to purchase a cottage with a garden large enough for his precious dahlias, and a convivial pub within walking distance. Ah yes, Tom stretched his toes to the warmth and counted his blessings.

Now the Snug was reserved for the Fun Club, the occupants chattering and laughing and shattering his sweet peace. The fact that the majority of the members were older than him did little to appease his affront, and he pondered gloomily on this unwarranted interruption of his tranquil life as he supped his pint from a barstool. A barstool, at his age!

The fault lay with Oswald, Chairman of the Club, Tom decided, and glowered across the bar as Oswald ordered drinks in his Sergeant Major's voice and herded his members to their seats. Recently retired to the village, he had immediately started organising. Tom didn't like to be organised.

As he meandered home, a solution sprang to his mellowed mind. He would join the Fun Club. He didn't relish the thought, but at least he could sit in comfort again and after all, he didn't have to participate in whatever they did. The next evening he braved the Snug and, fixing a smile under his scowling brow, approached Oswald.

"But of course, you're welcome, dear boy. Just pay your subscription and we'll hurry up the formalities."

Tom's heart sank further. "Formalities?"

"Well, you see…" Oswald tried to look superior, difficult when swaying slightly. "We do have a committee and they have to approve new members."

"Hmph!" Tom was annoyed. Approve him indeed, and then he spotted his chair, pushed into a corner, unused, and he relented.

"Well," he answered morosely, "there shouldn't be any problem there."

"We'll see." Oswald smiled coolly and turned away. "We'll be in touch."

Dismissed, Tom returned to the bar, his anger bubbling. Really, it was a bit much!

Two nights later, as he studied his emptying glass, the summons came. The committee were convening the following night. Would he report, promptly, at eight o'clock that evening.

It was a long twenty-four hours.

The committee were arranged in a semi-circle around him. He surveyed them suspiciously. He knew most of them, but tonight they appeared alien. Oswald cleared his throat and there was much shuffling of seats. Tom waited. Oswald stood and beamed around his Club.

"My dear members," he began pompously, "we are met here tonight to agree to the membership of young Tom Parker here." Tom winced. "I'm sure he will be a welcome addition and will bring new ideas for our entertainment." He laughed heartily.

Tom felt queasy. What on earth were they on about?

"We call it the Fun Club because we organise outings for fun every weekend." Oswald guffawed at his own wit. "Have to keep our minds active. I'm sure you're full of wonderful suggestions to share?"

Tom stared at him. His dahlias kept him occupied at the weekends and he certainly had no intention of sharing *them*.

"Has anyone any questions for dear Tom?" Oswald ignored Tom's silence and his gaze swung round the committee.

"Ah, Mr Parker." Miss Johnson, the club secretary, who had been writing avidly throughout, now raised beady eyes in a wrinkled face. "You live in that nice little cottage by the Post Office, I believe?"

"I do, ma'am." Tom drew down his eyebrows.

"Yes," she repeated, "such a nice little cottage." She smiled at him coyly, leaning her ample bosom on the table. "And of course, you're a widower." She giggled.

Tom's eyebrows lowered further and he glared repressively at her. He was very thankful for his single status. He had served his time in marriage and had no intention of doing a second sentence, but Miss Johnson obviously had aspiring thoughts on him and his nice little cottage.

"What do you anticipate contributing to the Club?" Oswald's voice was barely civil, but he didn't like the way Miss Johnson was simpering at Tom Parker. "I mean, Tom," he smiled thinly, "I take it you will join us in our outings? We have one planned for next weekend, in the country. We're all bringing a picnic."

"Well…" Tom was thoughtful. A trip to the country might not be so bad, he could always wander off on his own and he'd take his binoculars. Tom suddenly felt more cheerful.

"I'm very interested in birds," he ventured. "I enjoy bird watching."

"Don't we all!" An irreverent guffaw from across the circle brought a frown of reproval from Oswald, and Miss Johnson. Oswald smiled at her and straightened in his chair. "Thank you,

Tom, we'll let you know."

Grateful to escape, Tom scurried back to the bar.

"A pint, George, quickly."

George grinned. "Put you through it, did they?"

The beer frothed and Tom supped deeply before answering. "Silly idiots."

He hoisted himself onto the offending barstool and tried to think positively. It might be quite pleasant to be a member, help him make a few more friends, and trips to the country were few and far between now he had given up driving. If only there wasn't Oswald, and Miss Johnson. He shuddered.

He heard the scraping of chairs and increased chatter in the Snug. The meeting was obviously over. Gloom overcame him again. Miss Johnson didn't help his mood. Spotting him in the bar she scurried to his side. She was sure he'd be accepted. Looking at her, he didn't think he wanted to be, and looking at Oswald's disapproving glare as he called Miss Johnson back for her drink, Tom didn't echo her optimism.

"Another pint, George."

"You've caught the lady's eye, I see." George's own twinkled with barely concealed amusement. "Our Major won't like that."

Tom shot a questioning look across the bar and George leaned over and lowered his voice.

"Got designs on Miss Johnson, he has. Well, her semi, anyway. In lodgings himself, you see."

Tom sighed despondently. What sort of merry-go-round had he unwittingly stepped onto? Miss Johnson had aspirations on his cottage. Oswald had aspirations on Miss Johnson's semi. And all Tom wanted was to be left in peace in the Snug with his horsehair chair and the warm hearth.

The next day a letter was pushed through his letterbox. Oswald was happy to accept him as a member and they looked forward to seeing him in the Snug that night.

He went early. Pulling his horsehair chair to the edge of the hearth he ordered his pint, sat back and relaxed. Even Miss

Johnson couldn't douse his warm comfort and Oswald ignored him. He paid his fare for the outing.

On Sunday he clambered aboard the bus and claimed a seat by the window. His binoculars hung from his shoulder, his wild bird book filled his pocket, and he'd even managed to make a couple of sandwiches. He felt optimistic.

How Miss Johnson managed to secure the seat next to him he never knew and he felt most uncomfortable about the avenging looks directed through the seats by Oswald. Tom tried to concentrate on the scenery.

"Such a beautiful spot near the river, you'll love it." Miss Johnson touched his arm lightly and Tom wriggled uneasily in his seat. He hoped the journey wouldn't take too long. He wished Oswald would look the other way, and tried to smile in response to Miss Johnson. It was very difficult.

It was not easy to shake off Miss Johnson. Thoughts of a lone walk along the riverbank were reluctantly dismissed as, every time he tried to sneak off, she was there, pointing out birds for him to focus on. He lost interest. The afternoon seemed endless. He had hoped Oswald would relieve him of Miss Johnson, but Oswald appeared to be sulking. Tom sighed and longed to return to The Jolly Duck.

At last it was time to board the bus. By sheer force Tom grabbed a seat by the village butcher. He discussed meat avidly. Miss Johnson sulked. Oswald started to cheer up. Tom felt a wonderful sense of release and even the details of dissecting a pig did nothing to dim his spirits as they sped towards home.

Tom managed to avoid the next outing, sneaking into the Snug as the bus sped away and settling joyously into his chair, alone before the blazing logs for the whole afternoon. Bliss!

Tom wasn't sure how Miss Johnson came to tea that Friday afternoon. He supposed he must have invited her, for came to tea she did, but the actual asking remained a blank in his mind. Anyway, here she was, making herself quite at home. Tom was uncomfortable. Miss Johnson always made him uncomfortable. He wondered if Oswald knew and cringed. He sighed and went to put the kettle on. She stayed all afternoon. He began to wonder if he would ever get rid of her as he watched her demolish his favourite chocolate biscuits.

"Such a lovely cottage." Miss Johnson beamed at Tom and her eyes roamed the room as she stretched her toes to the fire. "So warm and homely."

Gloomily, Tom had to agree. He didn't like sharing his sanctuary, or his biscuits. At last she left and Tom closed the door hurriedly as she trotted down the path, a satisfied smile on her face. Tom wasn't smiling. He felt utterly miserable and somehow, trapped.

Miss Johnson's visits were becoming increasingly frequent. She didn't wait for an invitation; she just arrived. Tom felt hunted. He tried being unresponsive, he tried being rude and he even tried not being at home when she called. But somehow, she knew he was there and he was defeated. He thought of stopping away from The Jolly Duck, but long nights alone seemed intolerable. He was getting desperate.

Besides, there was Oswald. He didn't like the way Oswald looked at him and, although he staunchly believed himself not to be a coward, Oswald made him feel distinctly queasy. So did Miss Johnson. He didn't like the way she brought a pair of slippers, and left them, 'Just in case I drop in and it's raining'. They made him nervous. Big and pink and furry, they invaded his room and sat there, smugly, on the hearth.

So the days passed. Oswald fumed, Tom drooped, and Miss Johnson flourished. Thunder in the air nurtured the volcano smouldering in The Jolly Duck.

And so it was, one glorious day after torrential rain, that an eruption exploded in the Snug.

The members of the Fun Club had been for a quiet country walk, nothing too strenuous, just a casual amble through sun-drenched lanes admiring the early spring flowers.

"Delightful," murmured Miss Johnson.

Tom nodded miserably and concentrated his thoughts on his horsehair chair waiting patiently by the hearth, beer cooling in the barrel – the distant rewards of comfort. He felt swept along in a tide of submission. Sometimes he felt as if he were drowning, sometimes he wished he could! He wondered if he should move.

At last they turned back, Tom striding ahead and opening the Snug door with a flourish. As soon as he stepped over the threshold he knew something was wrong. Miss Johnson was beaming at his shoulder. The room had changed; it was a nightmare. George had spring-cleaned. Everything had been re-arranged and oh, horror, his chair had gone. In its place a black leather couch squirmed slimily around the hearth. He must be dreaming. Of course he was dreaming. He laughed, slightly hysterically, but he didn't wake up.

"Aren't you pleased, Tom? I persuaded George to clean the Snug up a bit, get rid of the ancient furniture. I knew you'd be overjoyed." Miss Johnson twittered happily on, mistaking his blank stare for joyous shock.

Tom's fighting spirit exploded and he lost control.

"Pleased, overjoyed? Damn you woman, where's my chair?"

Miss Johnson let out a frightened squeal, recoiling before his roar.

"Well…" She turned to Oswald for support and he put his arm around her shoulders protectively.

"There, there, my dear, don't upset yourself." Oswald frowned threateningly at Tom. "Don't you dare speak to a lady like that!" He thrust his face closer to Tom's. Miss Johnson simpered nervously.

"My chair, where is it?" Tom glared at Oswald and then at the shiny monstrosity in its place.

George intervened. "Just a minute, Tom, calm down, there's a good man. It's about time the place was done up and it was Miss Johnson's idea to buy the couch. She thought it would be cosier than your rickety old chair."

Miss Johnson nodded anxiously.

"It's only out the back," George continued. "I'll soon bring it in if that's what you want. The customer's always right!" Shaking his head George disappeared into the bar.

Tom looked at Miss Johnson with loathing and turned to the door. Without another word, he walked out.

"Funny fellow." Oswald rubbed his hands together heartily. "Always knew there was something odd about him. Poor chap, more to be pitied really." Oswald could afford to be generous.

"Now, my dear," he steered Miss Johnson towards the couch, "if you'd like to sit down I'll get you a drink, to calm your nerves. You've had quite a fright."

Miss Johnson smiled shakily and sank down, but she couldn't help admitting that leather was very cold to sit on.

Tom concentrated on his dahlias and it wasn't until he heard the news of the wedding that he ventured back into The Jolly Duck. The Snug was wonderfully empty and, lo and behold, there was his old horsehair chair in pride of place by the hearth. He glanced at the notice board and beneath the heading '*Fun Club*' read: '*Due to the extended honeymoon of the Chairman and his secretary, the Fun Club is postponed indefinitely. Please carry on enjoying yourselves without us.*' Tom grinned.

The next day Tom put a parcel on the doorstep of Miss Johnson's semi. The attached note read: '*From my hearth to yours. Congratulations.*' Inside was a pair of fluffy pink slippers, slightly worn.

Boxes

It was a beautiful box; hand carved, grained wood deeply polished. Ben couldn't resist entering the shop and leaning into the window to gaze at it again. The glass hadn't lied. Carefully he reached between the scattered miscellanea and lifted the box towards him. It felt like velvet to his touch, warm from the late sun slanting through the panes, welcoming.

"Can I help?" She moved silently behind him, smoothly elegant, an alluring smile lighting flawless features.

"Quite beautiful." His hands caressed the wood as his eyes lingered on her.

"Beautiful," she agreed. Her voice was melodic, gentle.

For a moment he forgot Cathy, forgot his reluctance to go home, to face the chaos left from the morning; he and Cathy racing to get to work, neither prepared to compromise. The flat was cold, the heating poor. A damp chill pervaded every room. Neither liked cooking, and the stale smell of take-aways clung to the hunched settee. Their dream home, conjured up in their final year at university, materialising in reality on meagre wages. Disillusion; tired voices raised in anger, blame ricocheting in arguments and ultimate desires incompatible.

He shivered as her hand touched his on the box, dissipating his anguished thoughts and emphasising his negative expectations.

"It's unique, antique," she purred, her eyes enticing him.

His hands explored the delicate engravings and her smile

embraced him. He knew he was being foolish, but his craving to possess overwhelmed him.

He was short of cash. The heating needed fixing. Cathy wanted to move. Neither dared admit their love was over.

They'd visited the show house only yesterday. Cathy had been thrilled. Bigger than her parents' beautiful house, newer, on an estate on the edge of town backed by green fields; for how long, Ben wondered cynically.

"It's so perfect!" Cathy had been enthralled, her hands clasped tightly and her eyes glowing, the glow that had once encompassed him being rekindled by a red brick box. Rows of red brick boxes, neatly laid out, matching, gardens prim and exposed, all uniform. The few completed houses were already occupied, new cars, grimy with building dust, decorating the drives; the garages full of hidden rubbish, empty computer boxes and old lawn mowers.

Unbidden, a tune started in his mind, '*Little boxes, little boxes, little boxes made of ticky tacky, and they all look just the same*'. He hadn't realised he was humming his thoughts out loud until Cathy glared at him.

He hated the estate. It wasn't Cathy's fault. She had grown up in this environment, her parents encouraged her in materialism and they shared her ambitions. He thought longingly of his own parents' terraced back-street home. Cosy, comfortable, loving, nothing to covet next door, just life to share.

He trailed after Cathy into the streamline kitchen. Sparkling, convenient, a haven for a busy wife and he shuddered. He saw the brochure on the table. The same brochure depicted every house on the estate. He thought of the brochure that bulged in his pocket. He had picked it up on a whim and spent days trying to pluck up the courage to suggest to Cathy that they had a holiday, before committing themselves to the endless tunnel of debt that this new house promised.

Africa! He longed to go to Africa. They were young enough. Plenty of time yet for settling into the rut, having children, starting a pension; plenty of time. And Africa beckoned. He hadn't yet had the nerve to mention it. He couldn't bear the thought of further rejection. Africa was an attainable dream, until Cathy said no.

So he still hadn't asked her and, as he looked around this immaculate kitchen, he knew he never would.

"We could afford a down payment," she had turned to him eagerly, "and if you ask for a raise?"

He hated the way her face froze into disdain when he shook his head. Hated the way her lips thinned and her heels clacked across the glossy vinyl. Slouching, he dug his hands into his pockets and followed her down the tarmac drive. His fingers curled around the brochure of Africa and he winced.

It hadn't always been so grim. They had been joyous students. So much in love; first jobs, excitement in a new world, together. Dreams decorated the flat, laughter eradicated the chill damp and love weaved a glossy perception of happiness. When did reality win? At what stage did the coldness permeate their snugness and cunningly devour their carelessly scattered love? He didn't know, couldn't remember.

The dreams vanished with the storms and he began to accept that life was like that. This morning had been no different.

"So, when can we find somewhere decent to live?" Her voice had been harsh.

"Later, when I get my promotion." Weariness had followed him from the bed.

"When!" Her bitter voice echoed in his head.

He shrugged and left. 'One day.' The futile words clouded his brain as he took the train to work. Work, that was all it was, a dreary slog through the days. A career in insurance had glowed through the future, fired by his imagination; and yet here he was, nothing more than a junior adviser in a large company. Was this how he wanted to spend the rest of his life, learning how best to insure it? Surely there had to be a better way of earning a living, something exciting, even unpredictable, a career that would make him glad to be alive. He had already worked out his pension and how long it was before he could draw it! What was the matter with him? Where had all his dreams gone? As he left the train he made a promise, today would be different. And so it was.

Today he had levered his head above the mire and taken a decision. He had approached the manager. It was time he moved on, moved up, updated his training, anything to alleviate this wretched rut of misery.

The manager was surprised but accommodating. He agreed. Ben had been there a long time, my goodness yes, he hadn't realised how long, but he was such a pleasant employee, he had got used to having him about. But yes, why not? Further training would enhance his skills; give him a chance to improve himself. Of course, why not? He'd look into it. Beaming, he waved Ben from the room. Ben had been elated and terrified.

Now, as he caressed the box in his hands, the adrenalin flowed and sensuality excited his fingertips.

"How much?"

She named a figure, quietly, so that it slipped into his head and didn't seem too outrageous.

"Maybe," he hesitated.

"I can put it by for you, until pay day?"

She leaned towards him and he let the waft of musk drift over his senses, inhaling deeply, allowing it to trigger long forgotten yearnings. He hadn't desired anything so much for a long time.

"Thank you."

Reluctantly he relinquished the box to her hold and her fingers brushed his, lingering, almost in promise. Such warmth, such comfort.

His step was light as he sped home.

It was only later that reality stepped in. What must he have been thinking of? A wooden box; he had put a deposit on a ridiculously priced wooden box, and what was he going to put in it for heaven's sake, his socks to keep warm? Because he certainly couldn't afford to pay for heating repairs now! Madness. He didn't confide in Cathy, but that wasn't unusual.

His eyes were critical that night. The flat was a mess. Cathy was a mess, untidy, almost slovenly, uncaring, unloving. Why was he still here, with her? He felt surprise at the question.

"What's the matter?" Cathy came and sat on the arm of his chair and smoothed his hair, offering peace. "Bad day?"

He thought of his interview with the boss, but stayed silent. Cathy would have been so pleased. Why not tell her?

"Do you love me?" He wasn't sure why he asked her that.

She looked startled and moved away.

"Of course." She looked uncertain.

"How about a holiday?" He smiled impulsively. "We could do with one."

"We can't afford it."

His smile slid away. He remembered a holiday. Laughter, fun, love; it seemed a long while ago. He thought of his box; he still had to find the balance to pay for that. But it consoled his mind.

It reminded him of a shoe box he had as a child, full of mementoes, dreams. He only had to open the lid to be transported into another world. He had snipped cuttings from magazines, foreign people, strange lands. He had sat on his bed and devoured the flat surfaces, his imagination talking to the children, feeling the hot sun, running from the wild animals. One day, he would travel and see these places. His mother had laughed.

"You go, my lad, go while you can, escape and enjoy yourself. Life will catch up with you soon enough! Run away and experience."

She would save special clippings for him, a faraway look in her eyes as she handed them over.

"Take care of them, Ben," she would whisper. "Take care of your dreams."

Perhaps he could recapture those ambitions; maybe, if he could find something exciting to fill the box, he could have a second chance at happiness. It was a symbol, he was sure of it, a symbol of hope, and his thoughts slid across the top of the carved lid to its present owner, and his heart leapt in anticipation.

He packed his bags and left as only a coward can, when Cathy was at work. His note was full of apologies and very cruel. Cathy wouldn't understand but, possibly, she would be relieved. He rented a room, dull but adequate, and unpacked. Then he headed for the shop.

Her eyes were richer, her smile deeper and he thought her more beautiful. She fetched the box from the back of the shop and he duly handed her the money. It was his. His future was here and now, within arms reach. He grasped his package and pushed the receipt into his pocket. He held her outstretched hand as a lifeline, tightening his grip as she flinched away.

"Are you free, after work? I should like to buy you dinner, to say thank you."

Her smile froze, her warmth melted in the blizzard of rejection. "I'm not free."

She turned away and he felt the cold blast of the open door as he stumbled out.

He placed the box carefully on his bed. So much care had been put into the carving, so much love into the polishing. And then he realised it was all surface seduction. Lifting the lid he saw the wood was unfinished, roughly hewn, and the box was full of rubbish, shredded pictures from a travel magazine. He stared at it for a long while, shrouded in despair.

Then, heaving himself from his gloom, he resolutely tipped the contents into the bin and carefully cleaned and buffed the wood. Polishing gently, his dreams slid nervously around the edge of his mind. Finally satisfied with the perfection of his box, he placed the brochure of Africa inside and closed the lid.

Loving Spirit

"**G**reat Gran Munchkin haunts my cottage!" I grinned at my friend Stella who was sitting opposite me in the coffee bar.

"Really?" Stella's eyes sparkled. "Oh, Carrie, what fun!"

"Well, it was like this..." Encouraged by her interest, I launched into the old family tale. "Great Gran Munchkin's ancestors, believe it or not that's her real name, came to this country from some remote island and settled, buying the cottage. Anyway..." I leaned across the table towards the enthralled Stella. "When she was only sixteen she was married off to a suitable suitor, although her love lay elsewhere!"

"It happened in those days!" Stella nodded wisely.

"Her marriage wasn't unhappy, but her heart always belonged to her one true love and, legend has it, she now haunts the cottage, hoping to find immortal fulfilment through her descendents!"

"Have you seen her?"

I shook my head. "I'm hoping," I replied solemnly. "I haven't been there six months yet, so she probably doesn't realise I've moved in. I'm sure she'll make herself known to me when she wishes."

Stella laughed. I didn't believe there really was a ghost of course, but the story was fascinating. It had been Mum's idea that I stay in the cottage for a while.

"Just until you get some money saved," she had suggested.

It seemed like a good idea. Only three miles from the town,

tucked away down a country lane that had not yet been spoiled by developers, the cottage offered me comfortable accommodation while I saved my wages, which weren't that good as yet.

Stella and I were junior secretaries in a thriving retail business but, until we proved our worth, the wages only just covered living expenses. Great Gran's cottage seemed an ideal solution.

"I must come and stay." Stella was enthusiastic.

"Of course, if you want to, you know you'll be welcome. But don't expect Gran Munchkin to appear to order. She's very fussy!"

There were plenty of tales about Gran Munchkin. She'd been a domineering lady, ruling her family with a rod of iron, but she also had a heart full of love and, when I looked at the portrait of her hanging in the hall, I was sure I detected a sparkle in the direct eyes, dark eyes that seemed to follow me up the stairs.

Stella was delighted with the portrait.

"Oh Carrie, how wonderful!" She clapped her hands and studied the picture.

Dressed in black lace Gran Munchkin sat ramrod straight, her hands demurely folded and her hair scraped into a severe bun at the nape of her neck. But her eyes were amused, as if laughing at her prim appearance.

"I'm sure she'll appear," Stella said with confidence. "There's definitely an atmosphere here."

Stella was into the supernatural. She reckoned it was because of her name, but I put it down to her romantic nature. Reality was always a problem for Stella. Whereas I was more down to earth, practical, enjoying life as it was and not expecting too much.

However, I must admit I warmed to Gran Munchkin and liked the thought that her presence was here to protect me. If she *were* around, she would certainly be friendly. But I really didn't expect an appearance to prove the point! I led Stella to a wooden rocker in the corner of the room.

"That was Gran Munchkin's favourite chair." I touched the arm gently and the rocker swayed to and fro. "My great grandfather carved it for her as a wedding present. She used to sit by the fire, rocking her babies to sleep. It was her special chair and no one else was allowed to sit in it."

Stella gazed in awe at the empty chair rocking gently to a standstill. She pushed the back with her fingers and set it in motion again, but she didn't sit in it.

"Too much aura," she commented and moved away.

I had to admit I sat in it once but I found the wooden seat uncomfortable and moved the chair away to the corner, preferring to curl up in the comfy armchair in front of the hearth, an open log fire adding to the cosiness. However, the chair was part of history and so it remained.

"Are you sure you've never seen a trace of her?" Stella urged.

"Well," I hesitated, "there was that night with Mark..."

"The Disaster!" Stella grinned.

"It was," I replied ruefully. But I couldn't put that disaster down to Gran Munchkin; could I?

I hadn't long moved to the cottage when I fell in love with Mark. He was everything my rather sheltered childhood had shielded me from, extrovert, wild and flamboyant. He didn't believe in working hard. He didn't believe in very much really, other than enjoying himself. His idea of a good time certainly opened my eyes.

I invited Mark to dinner. Whether I was nervous or whether Gran Munchkin was really watching over me I refuse to contemplate, but the oven wouldn't heat, the vegetables were soggy and my gravy congealed. Mark laughed unkindly and I was hurt and angry. When he insisted he heard someone moving about upstairs I yelled at him.

"Of course," I screamed. "It's a ghost! Didn't you know I have a ghost here, watching over me?"

"It's a pity you didn't let your ghost come and do the cooking, we might have been able to eat it – I'm off!"

He slung his jacket over his shoulder and slammed the door. I heard his motorbike roar away. He hadn't suggested I go with him and I was mortified. Several days later, when the tears had dried, I could look at him dispassionately. He wasn't a very nice person, I finally confessed to Stella, much to her relief. He didn't contact me again, so that was the end of that romance!

Since then the cottage had been peaceful and I'd come to put the disastrous meal down to misfortune. Certainly no hint of Gran Munchkin's presence pervaded the rooms with Stella present and, when we returned to work on Monday morning, Stella could hardly contain her disappointment. There hadn't been so much as a creak in the night and she was inclined to think I'd made up the whole story.

"Are you sure there's a ghost?" she demanded as we uncovered our computers.

"Of course not!" I laughed. "I'm just repeating the tales I've been told. No one's ever said they've actually seen Gran Munchkin!"

"Hmm." Stella looked at me doubtfully, but all thoughts of ghosts were wiped from our minds with the appearance of the new salesman. The manager, Mr Morgan, was showing him around. They stopped in front of our desks.

Mr Morgan beamed at us. "This is Tony, he's joining the team. Tony, these are our two young secretaries, Stella and Carrie, they usually type up the orders so you'll need their help. I'm sure you'll both make Tony welcome, girls."

Tony smiled and passed by to the next office. Stella and I stared at one another.

"Wow!" Stella's eyes sparkled and my heart sank.

I thought he was dishy too, but against Stella's blond vivaciousness my own dark looks seemed a little tame.

"He was certainly gorgeous," I admitted. "I wonder if he's got a girlfriend?"

"We'll soon find out!" Stella grinned.

And she did. He hadn't, and Stella forgot all about my haunted cottage as she tried to encourage Tony's friendship. He seemed quite nervous and I felt sorry for him when Stella's flirtatious manner obviously embarrassed him.

"Tone it down a bit, Stella," I said one lunch break. "The lad's obviously shy and you're frightening him to death."

"Rubbish," Stella scoffed. "Anyway, he's agreed to come to the staff dance on Saturday."

My hear sank, but on Saturday I dressed with care, applying more makeup than usual and sweeping my long hair into a fashionable style. I sighed when I saw Stella.

She looked stunning in a dress that hid very little of her perfect figure and I grinned ruefully as she grabbed Tony for the first dance. He caught my eye as he followed her onto the dance floor and winked. My heart did a quick flip and then I turned away.

I was surprised to feel his hand on my arm a little while later as the music slowed. He pulled me against him as we glided onto the dance floor.

"I've been wanting to get to know you for ages." He smiled down at me and I felt myself shiver as his arm tightened against my back.

"I thought Stella…" My voice tailed off as his eyes held mine.

"Oh Stella's great fun, a smashing girl, just not my type."

I grinned back at him and felt a delicious curl in my stomach. Stella wasn't going to be too happy about this situation but, for once, I felt confident. It was me Tony was attracted to; I was in heaven!

I have to admit that Stella was rather miffed when we discussed the dance next day, but her sense of humour soon returned and she wished me luck.

"Plenty more fish in the sea," she said and sighed.

I decided to invite Tony for a romantic dinner at the cottage.

"Watch out for Gran Munchkin." Stella laughed. "Remember Mark!"

I cast her a withering look and wished I hadn't confided in her. Tony was different. I was sure Gran Munchkin would approve, if, of course, I believed in her existence.

That Saturday I fussed around the kitchen, checking my menu repeatedly and muttering under my breath. I was a reasonable cook, I knew that, and with luck (and Gran Munchkin) on my side, I could produce an acceptable meal.

Tony arrived on time. I was nervous. I started romantic music playing and ushered him to the most comfortable chair in front of the blazing log fire. The table was laid beautifully, candles lit and wine at the ready. So far the food was cooking according to plan.

I needn't have worried. The meal was hot and appetising. Tony was complimentary and I breathed a deep sigh of relief. Not a board creaked.

We settled comfortably on the settee and finally I relaxed as his kisses sent shivers down my spine.

And then it happened, the sound of a movement on the stairs. Tony sprung away, startled.

"I thought you were alone?"

"I am!" I protested.

"Then who's that?" He was staring at the door and I sighed.

"There's no one there, honestly."

"Let's take a look." Tony was on his feet and I followed him to the door and up the stairs. All was silent. As we arrived back in the hall he stared at the portrait of Gran Munchkin.

"What a wonderful picture." He was studying her face and it seemed to me that Gran Munchkin was staring right back at him.

"That's my great grandmother." I paused. "Gran Munchkin. She's supposed to haunt the cottage, but I've never seen her."

"You don't see ghosts," answered Tony. "Or, at least, very rarely. You feel their presence, their aura."

"Do you believe in ghosts?" I was amazed.

"Amicable ones!" Tony smiled and took my arm, leading me back to the settee. "Wait here a moment."

I strained my ears as Tony disappeared once more into the hall, shutting the door behind him. Was that voices I heard? I shifted uneasily and then breathed a sigh of relief as a grinning Tony re-entered the room.

"Where have you been?" I demanded.

"Talking to Gran Munchkin." He smiled as he sat beside me and slipped an arm round my shoulders.

"It seemed to me that your great grandmother looked friendly, so I thought I'd better have a little chat, just to make sure. I didn't want her disturbing us again! And I was right, because, as I told her my intentions, I'm sure she winked at me."

I looked at him suspiciously, but his expression was serious.

"Hmm." I snuggled against him, aware of warmth coursing through my body. All last vestiges of nervousness left me. If Gran Munchkin approved of Tony then I had nothing to fear, did I?

I wound my arms around his neck as he kissed me again.

In the corner of the room the rocking chair swayed gently back and forth and I swear I heard a soft chuckle blending with the crackling of the logs.

Missing Data

"This data, Harry…" Jasper fluttered paper in the air above Harry's head. "This data is the key to your future."

Harry wasn't sure what 'data' was, but if Uncle Jasper said the paper was important then he'd better believe it! He tried to look intelligent and was relieved by further explanation.

"I've recorded your instructions for this new contract in simple steps. This way, you'll be able to understand your duties precisely. It's vitally important that every detail is exactly right. We can't afford any slip-ups."

Jasper towered over him, glaring at Harry to add weight to the importance of his words. A big man, his neck had concertinaed beneath the weight of his head and Harry viewed his uncle with awe. But then, Harry viewed most people with awe.

"Do you understand, Harry? I'm giving you a chance to show me what you're made of. If you fail me…" Jasper left the threat unfinished.

Harry shivered and nodded his head, his hair flopping over his forehead. Screwing up his eyes, he studied the sheet of paper Jasper had given him. This was his one chance to prove himself, so it was essential he follow the instructions to the letter. He had been a trainee in the family firm for nearly a year now and was anxious to progress from general dogsbody.

Not that he was unhappy. He enjoyed running errands, delivering and collecting mail; he met some very interesting people, and all the time he was gleaning knowledge so that, when his time came, he would be ready. Now was his time.

"Tea, Harry." Jasper had already returned to his desk and was frowning over a large map.

Sighing, Harry folded the paper reluctantly and went into the kitchen. Perhaps if he did well during this contract he would get promotion, maybe a desk of his own. Jasper might even take on another junior to make tea and fetch take-aways. The thought cheered him and he whistled through his crooked teeth.

Settled against the radiator with his mug, he once again studied his orders. He nibbled his nails studiously as he assimilated the steps outlined in Jasper's neat script. There were an awful lot of things to remember and his memory was inclined to be unreliable. Still, he could only do his best and hope that all would be well on the day.

"When does the contract begin?" he asked.

Jasper shrugged. "Soon I hope. There are a couple more details to clarify. I've got a meeting this afternoon and then, hopefully, it will be all systems go."

Jasper grinned. He was in a good humour. The firm had been suffering financially lately, the recession hitting everyone but, with this new contract under his belt, the future looked very bright.

Harry sat up most of that night, chanting his instructions like a mantra. He knew how important it was that he should come through this test successfully, his Mam had told him so.

It was his Mam who had got him the job in the first place, so, if he failed, not only would he be letting the firm down, but her as well. Jasper's sister, Rose, though tiny in stature, was the strong one of the family. Even when children the big, bluff Jasper had been intimidated by her ice-blue eyes and whiplash tongue. He had the brains, but she had the authority.

Harry could see her now, confronting Jasper with a courage that few possessed.

"Jasper," she had said sternly. "Harry's my only boy. You have to give him a chance."

"Why should I, Rose?" Jasper had whined irritably.

"Because he's family!" She had carried on in the same determined manner. "I know he didn't do no good at school, but he's a willing lad, and he'll learn under your guidance. Now his father's not around to influence him, I'm relying on you to teach him the tricks of the trade."

Jasper snorted and gave Harry a derisory look. Harry shrank into the chair and wished himself elsewhere, but, nevertheless, Jasper took him on and now was his big opportunity.

It was true he had been useless at school, but then, he hadn't understood a word the teachers had said, so what was the point in going? He had much more fun fishing in the brook or watching the *Dirty Harry* films at the cinema. *Dirty Harry*, now there was someone to look up to. Harry couldn't help a prickle of pride every time he heard his own name after that. Harry this and Harry that. He wondered if he'd ever reach the status of *Dirty Harry* or maybe even *Dangerous Harry*, now that would be something!

He muttered under his breath as he lay in bed. 'Step one, be on time. Step two, make sure you look the part, that is, best clobber. Step three…,' and eventually sleep claimed him for a few hours.

The next day Jasper was in an expansive mood, laughing and joking with his secretary and buying everyone cakes. Harry heaved a sigh of relief. He liked Jasper when he was being pleasant, he could think clearer when he wasn't being bellowed at.

"Harry," Jasper called him later in the day, "come here."

He led the way into the inner sanctum, an office that was only used for special clients, and shut the door.

"Right, Harry…" Jasper patted him jovially on the shoulder. "The contract's going ahead tomorrow, so we shall need you bright and early." Harry swelled with pride.

Jasper surveyed him up and down.

"Have you got any decent clothes?"

Harry nodded and then thought he'd better clarify Jasper's idea of decent.

"My jeans?"

"No, no!" Jasper shook his head. "You're going to be my chauffeur, Harry. A suit at least, or dark jacket."

"I've got me funeral suit," Harry answered doubtfully.

"Excellent." Jasper beamed. "And a clean shirt of course, maybe gloves."

"Gloves?" Harry looked startled. "I ain't got no gloves."

"No matter, you can wear a pair of mine." Jasper jotted a note on his pad.

"Can I have a hat?" Harry suddenly remembered *Dirty Harry* in a chauffeur-driven car, and the chauffeur had worn a very smart peaked hat. He was disappointed when Jasper shook his head.

"We can't run to a hat," he replied. "Just make sure you put plenty of water on your hair and slick it down. That'll do. Now, you've driven the BMW before?"

Harry nodded eagerly. Once, as a special treat, he had been allowed to drive the company car down the street. He remembered it clearly. It had been rather a comedown when he had returned to riding his old black bike. But now, he was going to be a chauffeur in the BMW. Harry grinned in sheer delight.

"Harry!" Jasper was tapping his fingers on the desk impatiently as Harry returned from his euphoric recall. "You've learnt all your duties?"

Harry nodded. "I drives you to the town centre, pulls up at the entrance to let you out." He frowned as he concentrated his memory on the numbered list.

"And then you drive round the block, pull up in a parking space just down the road – there's double yellow lines outside the main building where I shall enter – and when I come out from my appointment, you pull up alongside and you drive me away."

Harry nodded eagerly.

"It's very simple, Harry. Impressions are all important, and a chauffeur-driven car is a must."

Harry hardly slept that night he was so excited. The next morning saw him in his one and only suit, his shirt collar clean, Mam had seen to that, and his slicked hair dripping down his back. At the office he struggled into Jasper's leather gloves that made his fingers awkward, but he didn't dare complain, and then, there he was, seated at the driving wheel, his crumpled sheet of instructions carefully placed on the seat beside him.

Jasper got in the back, sitting like the Lord of the Manor, his leather briefcase on his knee, and Harry's heart swelled with pride. This was IT!

He scrunched the gears a couple of times as he negotiated the yard, but then they were on the road and Harry relaxed. He remembered his pep talk from Mam that morning as she had brushed the dust from his jacket.

"Remember, Harry, you're a natural driver. I've told you that before. It's the only thing you've inherited from your Dad, God rest his soul, but it's a useful one. Just concentrate and keep calm, and follow orders."

With a final flattening hand on his hair she had pushed him out of the door.

And now, here he was, driving like a natural. Jasper's relaxed expression in the mirror confirmed the fact and enhanced Harry's confidence.

He pulled up on the double yellow lines, keeping the engine running and staring straight ahead as instructed, while Jasper got out of the back door, straightened his tie and leaned through the window.

"Thank you, Harry, you may park now." Jasper spoke in the posh voice that Harry had heard him use sometimes on the phone and, besides a little nervous twitch, he didn't react, but pulled smoothly away from the kerb.

Doing a detour of the town he found a parking space a little way from the impressive double doors that Jasper had entered and settled down to wait. He checked his notes again. Jasper hadn't said how long he would be and Harry wondered if he dared put the radio on.

'Better not,' he muttered to himself. Nothing must distract his concentration. Impressions were paramount and he knew he had to be outside to pick Jasper up the minute he appeared.

It seemed a long while until the large doors opened and Jasper stood on the pavement, looking anxiously his way. Harry started the car immediately and cruised along the curb. A few seconds later the car door was pulled open and Jasper was in the back, his leather case bulging in his hand.

"Right, Harry, make it quick." There was a quiver in Jasper's voice but, before Harry could ask him if everything was all right, the engine stalled.

"What the hell...?" Jasper caught Harry's shoulder in a vice like grip. "For pity's sake, Harry, get going!"

His voice had gone croaky and Harry wondered if he was going down with a cold. He half turned to Jasper but the look on his uncle's face forestalled any speech. He tried the starter. The engine wound, spluttered and died.

"We've broken down." Harry calmly voiced the obvious, ineffectually pressing various switches.

"Broken down?" Jasper screeched. "You nincompoop, how can we have broken down?" His face had gone ashen and he was frantically trying to open the car door. "You've engaged the central locking, you useless lump. Open the door!"

Harry was studying the luminous gauges and pointed to a red flashing light. "There's something wrong there," he stated triumphantly.

"Do something, let me out!" Jasper was bouncing up and down in his seat. "You idiot. It's all your fault! Why on earth did I ever listen to your mother?"

At that moment a blast of alarm bells rang from the building that Jasper had recently emerged from.

"What on earth's that?" Harry covered his ears.

"The bank's alarm system, you useless piece of meat, you!"

"It's not my fault!" Harry wound the engine again.

Jasper groaned desperately and hugged his leather bound financial future to his chest.

Harry held up the now tattered instructions and carefully read them again as crowds started to gather around their car and outside the bank.

He shook his head in satisfaction. He smiled and waved the

grubby paper at the now blubbering Jasper. "It's not my fault," he repeated triumphantly.

And that was true, because nowhere in Jasper's instructions was there a step telling Harry to put petrol in the car.

Police sirens joined the cacophony of bells that echoed down the street.

Child of Destiny

I glanced through the peeling railings at the small country railway station. The buildings were in disrepair and the gardens uncared for, another landmark due for closure.

Shellack Wood. The sign was lopsided, the colour of the paint unrecognisable. In the distance I heard the train. Few people lived in this area now. The row of cottages along the road looked sadly dilapidated. Not many were occupied.

I didn't walk this path often. These days the woods weren't considered safe for a young woman on her own, but the sunshine and birdsong had beckoned and the remembered joys of my youthful explorations had overridden my caution. It was lovely to walk among the spring flowers, smell the budding trees, the newness of unfolding leaves.

I idled by the fence as the train neared. Slowly it pulled in at the unmanned platform. The door opened. A woman alighted carrying a child who kicked to be released. No more than two, he was chubby, dark haired and full of energy and fearless inquisitiveness. He toddled unsteadily from his mother as soon as his feet touched the ground.

"Danny, come here." Her voice was anxious, her face tautly lined around her thin cheeks. She looked weary, care-worn, a few years older than me, maybe not as many as her looks belied.

Briefly she raised her head. Her dark eyes met mine and I felt compassion and a sudden urge to reach out and ease her troubles.

As she caught the boy's hand and left the station she dropped a package from her loaded bag. I ran and retrieved it, calling after her.

"Excuse me."

She turned, her shoulders sagging, and waited.

"You dropped this."

She took the package with a brief smile. "Thanks."

"Can I carry something?" Impulsively I reached towards her overloaded hands.

She hesitated and then handed me a carrier bag.

"Thanks," she said again.

Her hair was long and dark, a similar colour to my styled short crop and she was the same height as me, but thinner.

"You live in the cottages?" The boy, Danny, was watching me curiously.

"The end one. It's cheap." She smiled, her face softening, the lines of worry easing from her face and I saw that she was pretty then. "It suits Danny and me."

"It's very isolated."

She shrugged. "As long as the train runs and we can get into town, we'll manage."

She opened a gate and turned into the path of the farthest cottage. I noticed the small garden was neatly dug. The curtains swung freshly against the sparkling windows.

"You'd like a cup of tea?" She unlocked the door and Danny toddled inside.

I followed her through to the tiny kitchen and put the bag on the table. Danny started to whimper.

"I'll get you a drink now, Danny." She reached for the kettle.

I picked up the protesting child and stared into the dark eyes so close to mine. He stared solemnly back and I felt my heart twist.

"Well, Danny," I spoke lightly, "and what do you think of living in the woods?"

"He's quite happy." His mother spoke defensively. "Of course, we shall have to move soon for him to start Nursery, but something will crop up."

"He's a lovely boy, aren't you, Danny?"

"Named after his father, Daniel." She sighed wistfully and I looked at her as Danny played with the beaded necklace at my throat.

She was reaching for mugs. "Same old story." She grinned ruefully. "I thought I knew it all; I had a good job, money, a nice flat. Then I met Daniel and fell head over heels in love. Life seemed so wonderful."

She sighed again and poured milk from a bottle. "I was pleased about the baby, once I got over the shock; it was then I found out Daniel was already married. When I told him, he didn't want to know me any more, wasn't interested in his child. Too corny to be true! How could I have been so dumb?" She turned away.

"I've never had time for those who went out with married men, and there I was. Ah, well. It's difficult sometimes, but we manage, and Danny makes it all worthwhile."

I looked at the child in my arms and tried to understand. My beads snapped beneath his grasping fingers and tinkled over the floor.

"Oh, Danny!" She lifted him from me and put him in a high-chair, thrusting a bottle into his reaching hands. He sucked greedily from it, his eyes never leaving my face.

"Don't worry," I said quickly. "They're not worth anything. But I wouldn't want Danny to think they were sweets and put them in his mouth."

She gave me a strange look.

We scoured the kitchen floor and gathered the beads. She looked at her handful. "They could be re-threaded."

I handed her the rest. "Not worth it." I turned away but I noticed she placed them carefully in a saucer on the sink.

I glanced at my watch. "I really must be going. Thanks for the tea." I brushed my hand over Danny's curls. "Be a good boy for your Mum."

His dark eyes stared at me, round and innocent over his bottle. His lips kept sucking.

"Perhaps I can all again?"

The girl smiled but didn't reply as she held open the door and I heard it close quietly behind me. The gate clicked shut and I looked back. The windows were blank, sombre now as a cloud hid the sun. Suddenly I shivered and hurried away.

A few minutes later I reached the outskirts of the town and the sanctity of my comfortable flat. I turned on the radio. I felt peculiarly morose, saddened by my encounter with the mother and child. I needed to dispel the gloom that hovered around me.

It was Saturday. Louise, one of my colleagues, was giving a party that night. It was sure to be a good do, her parties always were. Resolutely I turned my thoughts away from the lonely cottage and opened my wardrobe. What should I wear?

The encounter in the woods had unnerved me for some reason and, although the incident lingered in the shadows of my mind, I immersed myself in my job that I loved at the travel agents, partied and filled my life as hectically as possible.

It was several weeks before a Saturday, unmarked by plans and lightened by late summer sun, drew me in some inexplicable way towards the woods again. It was a lovely day for a walk.

I hurried through the trees. When I got to *Shellack Wood* station I noticed that workmen were repairing the booking office. The tin roof shone with fresh green paint. There was no sound of a train. I passed by and followed the road to the cottages.

An old man was digging in the garden next door as I walked up her path. The windows were grimy, no curtains danced behind the dim panes. Weeds throttled the flowerbed. The door was locked.

The man was leaning on his spade, watching me, as I turned round.

"Bain't no one there," he stated.

"So I see." I studied him. "Do you live here?"

He shook his head. "Only diggin' the gardens. Mr Jones, as owns these cottages," he jerked his head sideways, "he be doin' them up, thinking of letting them off agin. You'm interested?" He was watching me shrewdly.

I shook my head and smiled. "Not at the moment. I was just calling." I hesitated. "The woman and child who lived here, do you know where they went?"

He tipped his cap to the back of his head and scratched his forehead, puzzled. "Can't say as I do. Ain't been no one in these cottages for years, not since railway closed. Can't remember further back 'an that." He was staring at me and I felt uncomfortable.

"Course, now they'm resurrectin' all them railways, things be different, cottages will be wanted agin. Holiday homes for them townies, I 'spect," he predicted gloomily. "No one's interested in living here permanent, these days."

"They might be," I answered brightly. "If they're cheap enough and there's a train."

I turned away and heard his spade slice the undisturbed soil. I was scared. Surely I hadn't been imagining things? I had held Danny; he had seemed real enough! I fingered my necklace, and the broken beads had been real enough, easily replaceable of course.

The old man probably hadn't visited the cottages for years, he wouldn't have known of any short-term tenant and, of course, Danny would probably have started Nursery school by now. They'd obviously moved away.

I hadn't heard of this railway line closing and the tracks had never been removed, as so many had. There must have been a few trains running until now, when an increase was anticipated.

I was sorry. I would probably never see them again and I felt guilty somehow, as if I'd let them both down. I wondered if she had many friends. I doubted it. Perhaps I could have helped more? Now it was too late. I walked sadly home.

The party that night was as brilliant as ever. I swallowed a few glasses of wine and felt the familiar exhilaration, and the dismal thoughts that still persisted disintegrated. Life was such fun!

Louise caught my arm. "Welcome a newcomer to the area. He's living in digs at the moment, looking around, thinking of buying a house and he doesn't know anyone yet. I met him at Jane's party last night, took pity on him, and here he is."

Louise beamed up at the most gorgeous man I had ever seen. Dark, dark eyes and the sort of waving hair that left your fingers itching. Wow, was he something!

"Hi and welcome." I tried to keep my voice light but inside my stomach was churning.

"I'm sure I'm going to love it here!"

Louise melted away and the room seemed to slip into shadow. His eyes smiled deeply into mine and my heart catapulted.

He held out his hand towards me. "I'm Daniel."

I slipped my fingers into his grasp and fell head over heels in love.

Feet First

Megan woke to the clumping of her dead husband's boots on the flagstones in the room below. Backwards and forwards, pacing the early morning hours away.

"He canna' rest," Megan muttered and, pulling a shawl around her shoulders, she heaved herself from the bed. It was still dark but, as she peered through the window, she could see the sea mists lightening over the cliffs.

The spring mornings were chilly, but she knew she would get no more sleep. She might as well use the time usefully. Lighting her way with a candle, she peeked in at the children. James lay spread-eagled across the top of the bed, chubby arms thrown wide, his dark curls tousled from his restless sleep. Amy, a year younger, lay curled in foetal position, her mother's old shawl clutched tightly around her thin shoulders.

Megan smiled. They looked angelic in sleep, but then a line of worry creased her brow and she made her way to the kitchen.

The room was silent now. Samuel's boots rested on the hearth. Raking the embers, she threw on driftwood and the fire spat into life, warming her chilled fingers. Pulling the old wooden rocker nearer the warmth, she reached for the pile of linen. Threading her needle, she began hemming in neat, precise stitches. She had promised Lady Maddox she would have the cloths ready for collection today, and the extra hours of work would realise her promise.

⋆

When Betsy called for the cloths half-way through the morning, Megan had finished.

"You'll take some soup to warm you?" Megan smiled at the older woman as Betsy sank gratefully into a chair.

"Indeed I will," Betsy replied between laboured breaths. "Me legs ain't as strong as they was, that's for sure!"

"Can't her ladyship send one of them younger maids?"

"Oh, aye." Betsy accepted the dish with alacrity. "But they'm not reliable. Might go wanderin' off through the village, gigglin' with the boys, an' worse. Oh, no!"

Betsy took a slurp and Megan was relieved to see the colour return to her cheeks as her breath slowed. She was fond of Betsy; she'd been a real friend to her of late, and, Lord knows, she needed one.

Betsy had been housekeeper at the Hall for many years and Megan smiled now at her sharp tones. She knew Betsy ruled the staff with a firm hand, but she was also fair, and Megan was promised a place for Amy when the child was old enough.

"How's young James?" Betsy glanced out of the cottage window, seeing the two children playing on the rocks in the lea of the cliff. "Still wantin' to fish?"

"Aye, still wantin' to follow his father to sea. He spends all his spare time out in t'boat with Joe Fallows."

"Joe's a good man, he'll take care of James. Maybe even take him on eventually."

"Maybe," Megan sighed, "but I'd like James to have some schoolin'. I takes him to the village every mornin', an' then I find he's left afore afternoon's out. I was hopin'…"

Betsy shook her head. "If he don't like learnin', it ain't no good pushin' him. He can read an' write well enough?"

Megan nodded.

"There you be then." Betsy leaned back in her chair. "That's more'n your Samuel could do."

"I know. But I want James to learn a bit of thinkin', a bit of common sense."

"Not like your Samuel!" Betsy grinned.

Megan smiled sadly. "My Samuel was a good man, but he never gave a thought for consequences. Feet in first, I used to say to him, feet in first! Try *thinkin'* for a change."

Betsy nodded and they both sat, lost in thought.

"He canna' rest." Megan broke the silence abruptly.

Betsy raised her eyebrows.

"He canna' rest," Megan repeated. "At night I hear him pacin' the floor. His boots go clump, clump, clump; up an' down."

"He's tryin' to tell you somethin'." Betsy was thoughtful.

"What?"

"That he's sorry?"

"I 'spect." Megan smiled. "He always was, afterwards. Sell his fish, try a few drinks at the bar and then someone would upset him... His temper when he'd had a few was a sight to see! He never meant to fight, he was a big man an' he knew his punch was hard. He was always sorry – afterwards."

"Until the last time," Betsy added quietly.

"Aye." Megan stared into the distance. "He should have known better than to take on Jake."

Betsy nodded. "Jake's a bad 'un, always has been. 'Twas Samuel goin' on about the wreck he'd found, the bounty he'd reeled in along'a his fish..."

"What bounty?"

"Jake took pride in his salvagin', thought wrecks were all his; aye, an' some wouldn'ave been wrecks without a helpin' hand from Jake!"

"Shouldn'a said a word if there was any bounty. Perhaps Jake took it from him, after he knocked Samuel down?"

"Word is there was no treasure. Maybe Samuel found somethin', but the drink would make it treasure, an' then Jake would demand it, an' there you have it. A fight, only this time Samuel didn'a get up."

"'Twas the rock that split his head, not Jake." Megan sighed sadly.

"An' no one ain't seen Jake from that time to this, more'n twelve month now."

"I could've done with that bounty." Megan smiled wryly. " 'Tis no picnic bringin' up the young 'uns on my sewin' money. Still, we manage."

"Aye." Betsy fished in her pocket. "I forgot, I brought you this." She held up a piece of flowered cotton. "Her ladyship had it spare so I thought it might make a pinny for Amy."

"Oh, Betsy, that's lovely." Megan's eyes lit up. "She's growin' out of all she has; that'll make a lovely Sunday pinny."

"Aye, well, I'd best be makin' tracks." Betsy packed the cloths carefully in her basket. "They'm doin' out the bedrooms at the Hall; there'll be some curtains for stitchin'. I'll send the material down when it comes."

Megan nodded. "Please, Betsy, I'd be grateful. I've not much work left at the minute."

They parted with a hug and Betsy called to the children as she clambered up the steep cliff path to the village. Megan watched her go and started to prepare a stew for supper. She glanced at the boots by the hearth and wondered for the umpteenth time why her dead husband's spirit chose to pace her kitchen at night.

She knew that spirits sometimes couldn't rest. The Minister had told her so, but she had never heard of spirits donning their boots to do their haunting! Every Sunday, when she and the children attended the service in the Chapel, she prayed that Samuel's soul might rest in peace.

Now, as she kneaded bread and heard the children's laughter echoing with the call of the gulls, she stared at the boots. "What is it, Samuel?" she whispered. "What should I do?"

On impulse, she rubbed her hands on her apron and picked up a boot. Sitting in her chair, she rocked gently, holding the boot on her lap, and trying to reach Samuel. She slid her hand into the boot, feeling the leather warm from the hearth and, stretching her fingers, she laid her palm flat on the sole. The leather had almost worn through by the toe and, clasping her finger into the hole, she pulled the leather towards her. The sole came out easily.

Then she gasped. Something glinted in the heel cavity of the boot. She tipped the boot upside down. Gold coins tinkled onto the flagstones, rolling under the table.

Megan stared in disbelief. So Jake had gone away empty-handed after all! There were the rewards of the best catch Samuel had ever made, strewn across her floor.

Quickly she gathered the bounty, smiling to herself. So this was what Samuel had been trying to tell her. Imagine – she had been contemplating throwing the boots away to get rid of his haunting! She almost laughed out loud. She counted the treasure, unable to believe her good fortune.

Now, with careful management, she and the children would survive the lean years, until Amy and James were both old enough to earn their keep. The long nights of sewing by candlelight were over.

Dear Samuel. Her eyes filled with tears. Carefully she replaced the coins in the boot and put it neatly back. She dug her hands with renewed vigour into the dough.

That night she slept undisturbed, the polished boots on the hearth twinkling in the glowing embers of the fire. A waft of air flowed under the door, caressed the soft leather and, in a shower of sparks, floated up the chimney to the stars. In her sleep, Megan smiled.

Legacy of Sin

The town stilled as his horse crossed the boundary. Eyes swivelled, breathing halted. The horse looked tired, hardly raising its hooves from the dust, its head lowered on the slack rein as it passed down the centre of the main street.

The rider slouched forward, eyes focused, hardly moving. The long coat draped the travel worn boots and his dark hair was matted at his neck.

"Damon. It's Damon. He's back!"

Whispers travelled like a tickling breeze through the air and anticipating eyes watched.

The small town was short of excitement. Strangers rarely passed through with news and any that did were avidly pillaged for tales until they left, exhausted. Now one of their own was back, after so many years. Those who remembered his leaving had lost count of the time as life had gradually returned to normal.

"Damon is back!"

The news reached Annabelle from old Cyril. He thought she 'ought to know Damon was back'.

She stared in the mirror and pressed a stray hair into her coil. She brushed her cheeks, flushed from the news. At twenty-five she was considered past romance, but the bloom of youth still sparkled in her eyes and her trim figure hadn't changed.

*

There had been romances of course; many had courted her. But none had won her heart or inspired her to give up teaching the local children in the school. She had been glad of her father's training. Modern in his outlook, he'd taught her well and, after his death, she'd given her love to the children. She still missed him sorely. They'd been close. Her mother's early demise had strengthened the bond between them, and she missed his laughter and love.

Now, as she smoothed her appearance, her heart was racing. She stared into her own wide eyes in the mirror and the message there was unmistakable.

Damon was back, and she hadn't realised she'd been waiting for him.

When he came to call she was at the height of anticipation. Each day she'd worn a clean dress, braided her hair and tidied the small room. Cakes cooled and the kettle stewed on the fire. She was ready but, when the knock came, she found herself shaking so much it was difficult to lift the latch.

"Damon."

"Annabelle." He was sprucely dressed, boots polished and his hair slicked neatly. He looked older, but then he was, Annabelle reminded herself. After all, he had been only a few years younger than her father.

But his blue eyes still twinkled, although a look of anxiety now dimmed the sparkle as he waited for her reaction.

"Come in." She held the door wide and was surprised at her calm voice. He sat by the fire stretching his long fingers to the warmth.

"I wasn't sure I'd be welcome." He gazed round the cosy room. "It's good to be back."

"Of course you're welcome." Annabelle busied herself with brewing tea.

She had only been a child when he left, but she remembered the storm of anger in the cottage, her mother crying quietly and her father roaring in his temper, as he was wont to do. She hid behind her mother's skirts until she was pulled from the room and cuddled in the kitchen, her mother rocking her on her knee, sniffing as the tears dried.

The door slammed and Damon was gone. His name was never mentioned again and Annabelle was too afraid to ask. The man who held a place in her young heart, swung her onto his shoulders and told her tales of travelling the west, had erupted from her life in a cloud of fear, and gradually his presence faded and life returned to normal. But she never forgot; and now he was back.

"It's been a long time." She placed the mug by his side and sat opposite, studying his face.

"It has." He sipped slowly.

"Father died."

"I heard. I'm sorry." He sighed. "I should have come back sooner, only I wasn't ready and now…, it's too late."

She waited, afraid to speak of the past.

He reached in his pocket and took out a small bag. Fumbling with the strings he tipped the contents onto the table. Annabelle stared. Gold nuggets twinkled in the light and she put a hand to her throat.

"Where did you get that?" Her voice was a mere whisper and he smiled wryly at her expression.

"Don't worry. I came by it honestly. But it's taken a while." He watched her but she didn't speak.

"It was for your father, to repay my debt. But I waited too long."

"You owed him money?" It was the first time she had heard an explanation for the argument.

He shrugged. "Not exactly. The debt I owed him was too great to ever repay, but I hoped the gold might soften his heart a little and allow forgiveness."

He sighed. "I missed him sorely. Our friendship was too precious to gamble with. I learnt that lesson too late."

"What happened?" The question that had been in her heart for so many years finally exploded.

He touched her cheek with her hand. "Your mother never told you?"

She shook her head. "Father was so angry. It was a long time before there was any happiness in our house again. Mother wouldn't talk about it, and then she died."

"Was she unhappy?" His voice was very quiet.

Annabelle smiled gently. "I think she found peace at the end, she was very ill for a long time. My father nursed her untiringly. They loved each other so. But he survived the pain and he had me. We became very close."

He nodded. "He loved you."

"We had some good years and then he went too."

"And now?"

"I've made a life here. I have my home and I teach in the school. I love the children."

"None of your own?"

She blushed and shook her head. "I've never grown fond enough of a man to consider marriage."

'Until now,' her heart added.

"Where did Damon come from?" she had asked her mother once. Her mother smiled and stroked her hair, shrugging her shoulders.

"He rode into town one day." She laughed. "He asked your father for a job at the school. For some reason your father took to him, although he was a lot younger of course, and they worked well together. Between them they built up a good school. The children actually wanted to learn."

She laughed again and Annabelle accepted Damon into her life as easily as her father had done. It was not difficult. He was fun and smiling and good, spreading warmth wherever he went. The town's people took him under their wing and many forgot he hadn't been born in one of the wooden houses leaning into the hills.

★

They sat in silence for a while, the gold glinting in the firelight, each lost in past thoughts until, rousing himself from his memories, Damon rose.

"I must leave you, Annabelle. It would be unseemly to remain here after dark."

She blushed again and took his hand. "It was wonderful to see you again." Her voice was wistful.

He scooped the nuggets into the bag and tucked them away. "These were for your father." He stared down at her. "Now they are yours."

He held up his hand as she started to protest. "I'll deposit them in the bank. Spend them on what you will."

"I couldn't." She was alarmed.

"Of course you could." He laughed. "Buy some new dresses, build a new school. Whatever you choose."

She shook her head vehemently and he took her hand, kissing the palm.

"We'll talk about it again. Will you walk with me tomorrow, by the river?"

She nodded, confused. The river was an old haunt they had explored together but the money had frightened her. Damon by himself was unsettling, but Damon and a bag of gold nuggets were too much for her to cope with.

She sighed as she watched him from the window. His swinging gait was warmly familiar and her heart lightened as she thought of the morrow. There was so much more to discuss and at least he hadn't left the gold on the table.

She smiled as she thought of one of the neighbours calling and seeing her wealth. That would certainly set the tongues wagging even more, for undoubtedly they were clacking endlessly at Damon's return. And the fact that he had called on Annabelle when she was alone in the house would be the cause of some tutting and probably warning reposts.

As she prepared for bed and pulled the drapes, her thoughts sped back over the years when her young life was full of love; father, mother, Damon, all had loved her, laughed together and worked together, opening the small school where she now taught, her father sharing his books and Damon teaching the children the crafts of woodworking and practical living. It had been a wonderful venture, and life, until the storm. A tempest that had wrought them all asunder, and she still didn't know the cause.

But Damon felt it could be mended with gold. She wondered how her father would have reacted to the nuggets and she had a feeling they would have followed Damon down the garden path as he was evicted once again from the house. Perhaps it was as well Damon hadn't returned sooner, and then she felt guilty at her thought.

Sighing, she snuffed the candle and settled into uneasy slumber.

The next morning Damon proffered his arm and they walked sedately across the common to the river. Annabelle felt the eyes of her neighbours following them but she smiled brightly, her fingers clasping the sleeve of his coat. They spoke little.

The sunshine was warm on her back and Annabelle let out a sigh of relief as the trees closed about them and birdsong penetrated her thoughts. They were alone. The river tinkled merrily over the stones and she had a sudden longing to dip her feet in the cold water and let the fishes tickle her toes. It had been a long time since she had been a carefree child and memories danced amongst the grasses.

They found a fallen tree and sat on the rough bark.

"Nothing's changed." Damon sounded surprised as he looked around.

"Rivers don't change." Annabelle smiled. "Nature has a way of carrying on without us. I doubt our presence makes little impression over the years."

"True." Damon turned to look at her. "You've changed."

"I've grown up."

"You certainly have. And very beautifully, I might add."

Annabelle blushed and looked away.

"You've never married?"

She shook her head.

"That's a pity. You'd make a good mother."

She laughed. "After dealing with the children at school, I'm not sure I want to."

"With the right husband?"

"Maybe," she answered softly.

"Where did you get the gold?" she asked.

He shrugged. "It took a long time. Prospecting, digging, sifting, and then Lady Luck smiled and I found a seam. There's more to come. I've bought some land, built a small house, and I'm still digging."

"Far away?"

"Many days of travel."

"You'll go back?"

"Of course, it's my home now. There's a grand town growing nearby, all settlers, good folks. It'll be a prosperous place and happy I hope. I'm enjoying building a new life."

"But you came back?"

"I'd saved enough. I was hoping to settle my debt to your father, receive his forgiveness before it was too late." He sighed. "I'd heard you mother had passed on from a traveller but I'd hoped to see your father one last time."

"What did you quarrel about?"

There was silence for a while.

"I took something of his, something very precious, something I had no right to steal."

"You, steal?" She was amazed.

He nodded.

"Was it worth that much gold?"

"Far more; more than I can ever dig up. But I thought the willingness to make amends might soften his heart. Your parents gave me a wonderful life and I abused their trust."

"I'm sure Father would have forgiven you."

"Did he ever speak of me?"

Annabelle shook her head regretfully. "No."

He sighed deeply. "I wouldn't have expected him to. I was too cruel. But he was happy again?"

"Yes. He and I made our happiness. And he had the school. He loved his books. Even at the end, when he was ill, he was still training me to take over."

"You run the school alone?"

"I have help, but it's not always enough. The boys could do with manly guidance." She glanced at him wistfully. "You were always so good with words. The children would welcome your advice."

Damon shook his head. "They'll learn in their own time. My time here has gone. Pay one of the old men, a wise one, with the gold I brought. Make my brief pilgrimage back worthwhile. I've left the gold at the bank in your name. Use it as you will."

She shook her head. "I've no use for gold! How would I explain such wealth?"

"A gift from your father, left in trust with me. I've only just heard of his demise, and immediately journeyed to fulfil his wishes."

She thought for a moment. "I suppose I could say that, if you're determined."

"I am."

"But would Father approve?"

"How could he not approve of a kindness to his daughter, a gift to his beloved school?"

She was silent, her thoughts uneasy.

"When do you leave?" She touched his arm.

"Soon."

He stood up and reached for her hands. Drawing her close he gazed into her eyes. "I've missed you Annabelle. But you've grown into a fine woman. Your father did a wonderful job."

"I've missed you too, Damon." Her heart was fluttering. She had to be brave, as her father had taught her, honest with herself and Damon. She didn't want to lose love again, so suddenly had it returned.

"I love you, Damon. Take me with you."

She blushed at her forwardness, but Damon didn't withdraw from her clasp. His eyes, as he gazed deeply into hers, were full of tears.

"I love you too, Annabelle." Her heart leapt, and then was shattered.

"But not as you think you love me. You are so precious to me and I'm very proud of you. When my home is complete I'll fetch you to see it, but only for a visit."

"Do you love another?"

He was silent for a moment and then nodded.

"There was another." His voice was husky and his fingers gripped hers tightly.

She waited, holding her breath, and she felt her future lay in this moment of truth.

"You see, Annabelle, my dear, dear child, I have only ever loved one woman; and that was your mother."

Cake Comfort

I arrange my fruit cake carefully in the middle of the white doily on the glass plate. The white enhances the deep colour of the mixture. Perfect. I see Janice Laurence bearing down on me and I groan.

She has won every cake competition in the village since competitions started! She's afraid that, as a newcomer, I might oust her position. Her anxious expression fades and a gleam of triumph lights her eyes as she examines my pièce de résistance.

"Ah, Melanie, how nice that you've entered." She trails a manicured fingernail a fraction from the outline of my offering.

"Hmm." Her smile is malicious. "Slightly overdone?"

She sails away, confident in her unchallenged role.

My cake is more than overdone; it is definitely burnt around the edges. But I know that inside, it is squishy and delicious. It took me years to find the perfect oven setting for this particular creation and I know it will win.

You see, I have insider knowledge – I know the judge.

His name is Mario; now. Mario, the flamboyant master chef of the television series. Mario, with his black eyes and curling locks; his charisma that captivates the unsuspecting housewives, that unspoken invitation in his eyes that makes his programme a winner.

Mario is going to judge the cake competition this year. I've entered my cake under a pseudonym.

*

I first met Mario in the local chip shop. It had been a long day at work and I was hungry. I couldn't face going home to my cold flat and equally cold sandwiches.

"Cod, chips and mushy peas, please." I stared at the tall man at the fryer. He was new. I gazed into his deep sleepy eyes, almost covered by thick waves of dark hair, a white cap balanced precariously on the top and...

No, I didn't fall head over heels in love! Not that evening. His overall was vast and greasy, perspiration dampened his face and hair, and his eyes were red rimmed from fat fumes. Besides, I was hungry and tired and romance was the last thing on my mind.

It was a busy month. I called at the chip shop regularly. Mario smiled at me, his smile wider with each visit.

Then, to my horror, I realised I had put on weight. Scales do not lie, however much I suck in my breath. Searching for an enjoyable form of exercise, I hit on the local dance nights. Anything was better than the gym!

Now, there, I did fall in love, irrevocably and intensely. Mario, whirling around the dance floor, in tight jeans and a snazzy shirt, with hardly a hint of chip smell, was as enticing as his cod.

Of course, his name wasn't Mario then. He was plain Martin Pike. But I fell in love with him anyway and soon I was getting an extra piece of batter with my supper.

Inevitably, he moved into my flat and we would sit on the sofa, his arm around my shoulders while I listened to his dreams.

"One day, Melanie," he said, "one day, I'm going to be a top chef. One day I will be famous and I will be rich."

I wondered what had happened to the 'we', but I didn't comment, then. And there was very little evidence to show he could cook anything other than cod and chips. I was the cook then, with good old-fashioned cooking that kept us healthy. I had always been a plain cook; roast dinner and three veg. And fruit cakes; oh, how he loved my fruit cakes.

It gave me confidence, knowing I was providing the food. Whatever his aspirations, his stomach nurtured his love for me and, of course, he still treated me to fish and chips once a week.

He was lucky, my Martin. A new restaurant opened in town and Martin sweet-talked his way into the chef's post. My cod and chips went back to normal size.

That was the beginning. Give Martin his due; he had a flair for fancy cooking. He also had a personality that could woo the hardest complainant. He convinced the customers his food was the best, even if the dish was a disaster.

The restaurant was a success. London beckoned and London won. We moved. The dreams still contained a lot of 'I's and one day I queried this. I had managed to get a job in a burger bar, clearing tables, but somehow it didn't compare with Martin's lifestyle at the swish hotel where he now worked, and I hoped I might become a lady of leisure as his prosperity increased.

"Of course, chèrie, we will always be together." Martin had adopted an accent.

I wasn't sure whether it was meant to be French or Italian, but it didn't seem to matter. And he changed his name to Mario. That took a bit of getting used to.

Suddenly, he became critical. His eyes would sweep over me, and not with love. I wasn't keeping up with his rise to fame.

The only thing about me he still seemed to love was my cooking. Despite his flamboyance in the kitchen, his stomach made him a fish and chip man. He still loved my fruit cakes, and I had discovered, rather unfortunately in my opinion, that he liked them burnt. 'Crunchy round the edge and soggy in the middle' would send him into raptures in the early days of our partnership and even now, in those heady days in London, my cake could melt his heart.

But he was home less and less. He applied for, and got, his own television show. He was a success. I went to the soirées after each show, at first. Then I got fed up with the fluffy half-clothed bimbos that hung onto his arms, his words and goodness knows what else!

The crunch came when an itty-bitty bra appeared under my pillow. There was no way my cod and chip proportions could have worn that, whatever Martin said. So it was goodbye Martin. Mario had won.

I cried a little, nurtured my bitterness and sued a little, and ended up leaving London and living a comparatively easy life in a small cottage in the village to which I now donated my cake for the competition.

You see, I have one more chance to wreak sweet revenge on the man I gave my heart to; one more chance to try and ease the suffering that his constant appearance on television evokes in me.

The great Mario arrives. I hide behind dark glasses and a floppy sunhat and watch as he smiles and woos the housewives. How they love him, the television chef, the dashing hero of their dreams, every one wishing him flouncing into their kitchen, sweeping them into his arms with a flurry of sifted flour. Martin is a brilliant actor. Mario is now honed to perfection.

I watch him covertly as he tries the cakes, the cut wedges sampled amid explosions of ecstasy from his mouth. I see his eyes widen as he reaches mine. For a moment he frowns and studies the name card. His brow clears and he smiles. He eats the whole slice. No expletives here, just a look of sublime satisfaction on his face.

I grin and wait for the verdict. Janice Laurence's face is a picture as I step smartly towards the platform to receive first prize. So is Mario's as he hands me the silver cup.

A look of horror sweeps over his face for a moment before he smiles, tightly, his black eyes full of panic. He holds my cake before him. I smile into the flashing cameras. I see the London press have accepted my invitation and the hacks are dribbling at the impending scandal. This is not just a little village 'do' after all!

Mario, the great chef, has chosen a burnt cake as the winner. I grin as I visualise the headlines. I have a feeling that, after this, his credibility will be deep fat fried!

Just an Accident

"**D**oes Ellie know I'm here?" Susan's voice was anxious as she gazed down at her daughter, serenely unconscious in the hospital bed.

The doctor shook his head. "We don't know. We do know her mind is still active."

"She might be able to hear us." Susan's voice was hopeful.

"Possibly."

Since the car accident a week ago Susan had held long one-sided conversations with Ellie. She sighed.

The doctor patted her arm. "Go and rest. We'll phone you as soon as we see any sign of change."

Susan nodded and stood up. "I have to believe she knows I'm here, that we all visit, her father, and Peter of course…"

"Of course." The doctor's voice was soothing. "When she recovers, she'll tell us. She may be dreaming, remembering. Sometimes patients relive their past; sometimes, but not always. She might be able to hear your voice, just unable to answer. We have to hope."

Susan was surviving on hope. It had been such a silly accident, such a silly quarrel, Peter said, and Ellie had driven off in a temper. Susan couldn't blame Peter. He loved Ellie so, but Ellie was headstrong, independent. She wanted her freedom for a while longer and look where her flight had landed her! Peter wanted to marry her, shield her from hurts, and Ellie wanted to apply for a job by the sea. She loved the wild expanse of ocean, loved the freedom of the waves…

Ellie could smell the sea as soon as she stepped off the train. Tangy salt breezes lifted her hair and brushed her cheeks. She took a deep breath and smiled. When she had seen the vacancy advertising for a receptionist at the Castle Hotel, overlooking the beach at Chimera Bay, she had applied enthusiastically.

Her parents were doubtful at first but, as she pointed out, she was twenty-two and had never been away from home.

Working locally had its advantages and, of course, there was Peter, but now she felt the need to spread her wings and Chimera Bay was only a few hours away.

When she was offered the job, her parents relented and wished her luck. She wished Peter could have done the same.

Their relationship had been exciting at first, but now it was so predictable, so comfortable that, although Ellie was deeply fond of Peter, she longed for something more.

Peter didn't understand. The day she left they had a blazing row and she stormed away, anger and tears blurring her vision, her head aching painfully with his constant recriminations.

But, once on the train, her anger evaporated and the pain in her head receded; now here she was, on the verge of an exciting new life.

Castle Hotel was a majestic building, built from the castle ruins, ancient stone walls surrounding the prolific gardens, the wide windows allowing a panoramic view of the bay.

The doors slid quietly open as Ellie entered. The taxi driver followed with her cases.

A man was at the reception desk. Ellie had a brief impression of dark curls and a thin tanned face and then he raised his head and dark eyes met hers. A smile curved his full mouth and he sprang from behind the desk. Tall and lithe, he grabbed Ellie's hand in a firm grip.

"Ellie! I'm David. It's good to see you. Welcome to the Castle Hotel. I'll show you to your room."

Ellie had little time to draw breath before he took her cases and headed up the stairs.

"Thank you." She looked round her room in delight. Elegantly furnished and comfortable, she knew immediately she would be happy here.

"Thank you, David," she breathed as he deposited her cases on the floor.

"Unpack and settle in," he ordered. "Tea is in the kitchen at three, and then I'll show you around."

Ellie settled into her new life at once. She felt at home and her previous existence seemed a long distance away. She wrote to her parents, a letter full of bubbling joy and excitement, but she didn't contact Peter.

Her job was interesting, varied and not too arduous. David was on hand with advice and, on her days off, he took her to explore the surrounding countryside, fed her at small seashore inns and, before long, she knew she was in love. She knew instinctively that David felt the same way.

It was her day off and she and David were lazing on a small, secluded beach not far from the hotel. The hot sun had robbed them of strength and, when David slowly kissed her, it was deep and beautiful.

Gently he slipped his signet ring onto her finger. "Until we can buy the real thing," he whispered. Then he kissed her again.

She gazed at the gold band with its precious initials delicately entwined and her happiness was complete.

That night she lay in bed and contemplated the future. It stretched before her in a golden passage of time. Smiling, she slipped into sleep.

It was in the early hours that she awoke with a low moan. Her head was throbbing. Pain shot behind her eyes and she couldn't get her breath. Gasping, she struggled out of bed, forcing herself to inhale. She was suffocating. Her head thrummed and pain blurred her vision.

She had to have air. Gulping, she stumbled down the stairs and out through the side door. The cool night air was heaven against her hot forehead.

She crossed the dewy grass and sank onto a bench, clutching her throbbing head in her hands. The soft shush of the waves breaking on the pebbles calmed her as she desperately tried to breathe. Slowly does it, inhale, exhale.

It was painful and her head hurt, oh, how it hurt! She moaned and curled her head downwards into her lap.

The pain increased. Lights flashed in her vision, blinding her as the pain threatened to engulf her and become unbearable. Blissfully she sank into oblivion.

"Ellie moved!" Susan's voice was excited.

The doctor leaned closer. Ellie's father was hovering uncomfortably in the background.

Ellie heard a great rush of sound and felt the pain in her head again. Would it never stop? She groaned and opened her eyes. She saw her mother, her father and a man in a white coat.

"Where am I?"

"In hospital, dear." Susan's eyes filled with tears. "You had an accident, but you're going to be all right now."

"An accident?" Ellie was scared. Where was she?

"Where's David?" She tried to move.

Her mother looked startled. "David?"

"I want David. Where is he?" Her voice rose and the pain started in her head again.

With a moan she sank back onto her pillow. She felt a prick in her arm and then blessed darkness descended.

The next time she woke she felt more alert. She remembered she hadn't mentioned David to her parents. She'd been waiting until her visit home. Quietly she twisted the ring on her finger.

"Mum."

Susan smiled at her. "How are you feeling?"

"Awful!" Ellie winced. "Where's Dad?"

"He went home to get some rest. He'll be back soon."

"How long have I been here?"

"Ten days. Can you remember what happened?"

Ellie shook her head. It hurt. She remembered the day on the beach with David, going to bed and then... nothing, until the pain in her head and... this.

"You had an accident in your car."

"Car?" Ellie was confused. She hadn't taken her car to Chimera Bay. "Whose car?"

"Your car, dear. You went to see Peter and...," Susan hesitated, "I gather you had a row and then you drove off. You hit a tree."

"A tree?" Ellie was beginning to panic. Nothing made sense.

She gave up and slipped back into sleep. When she felt better she would understand what had happened.

The day Ellie went home to her parents' house she was frightened. She said little. No one seemed to know what she was talking about.

Her job at the Castle Hotel, David; everyone thought she'd been dreaming. She had been thinking of taking a job on the coast, that was what she and Peter had rowed about, so her mother said... Maybe it had been a dream; because where was David? And then she felt the cold ring on her finger, engraved with David's initials, and she knew it couldn't be a dream. But what had happened?

Peter was consumed with guilt. She'd told him she wanted some freedom and he'd been angry. She rushed out of his house and had an accident. He blamed himself. Ellie didn't want to discuss it.

Ellie recovered slowly. She bought a map of the south coast. Chimera Bay wasn't marked. She couldn't remember exactly where it had been located and she hadn't had time to explore nearby towns.

She knew she'd taken the train. The ticket office had no record of a train to Chimera Bay. She rang Directory Enquiries. There were plenty of Castle Hotels, but none at Chimera Bay. Only the ring on her finger convinced her that David had existed.

She woke one morning feeling better. The sun was shining and she was filled with optimism. Today she would be positive, today she would take a train to the coast and she would stay there until she found the right Castle Hotel and David.

Hurriedly she packed a case and told her parents her plans. They were horrified.

"You can't!"

"I am."

She opened the front door and ran down the path. The hastily summoned taxi had turned and was waiting. Ellie rushed into the road. Susan screamed.

The car coming the other way didn't have a chance to brake. Ellie felt the blow against her case and she was pushed to the ground. She felt the pain as her head hit the road and she groaned.

She heard tyres screeching, shouting, doors banging, but the pain in her head was receding…

She was all right. Her case must have taken the full force of the blow. The sun was still shining, a bright golden glow above her. If she ran she could still catch the train.

The ticket office was no problem today. Triumphantly she smiled as she read her destination in bold black letters, Chimera Bay. The salt air was like nectar as she alighted. The same taxi sped her to the Castle Hotel.

David was behind the desk.

"Ellie!" He ran towards her, his arms outstretched. "Where on earth have you been? I've been worried sick!"

Ellie smiled and gave herself to his embrace, feeling the glow of his warmth, his love. She knew she would never leave David again. This time, she had finally come home to stay.

Later, she would tell him what had kept her from him for those long days; but that wasn't important right now.

"I thought I'd lost you." His voice was muffled in her hair.

"No, David." She held him tightly. "I didn't mean to go away. It was just an accident."

Quietus

When Amelia Smith, widow, met Timothy Townsend, divorcé, at the local Singles Club, she was immediately impressed. As they talked she discreetly studied his expensively cut suit and elegant gold wristwatch.

She was slightly disconcerted when she learned that he had been divorced twice but, when he explained about the terrible life both wives had led him, finally deserting him for equally unscrupulous bounders, she forgave him. It wasn't his fault that his judgment of women so far had been misguided. After all, he was a man, and Amelia's opinion of men had hardly altered since her father had warped her viewpoint. But, she had assured herself, she was open to persuasion that there may be a man out there who could match her expectations.

Very soon she convinced Timothy that evenings together would be far more equable if he called on her in her neat little cottage on the edge of the village. She had chosen the cottage for its solitude and peaceful surroundings: green pastures and majestic trees. She craved tranquillity and the cottage was far enough away from neighbours to eliminate all intrusive noise.

"Timothy, my dear," she murmured. "I do so dislike our relationship being monitored by the other members of the Club. I only went there by chance. Feeling a little lonely, you know?"

Timothy agreed with her heartily. Well, what could possibly compare with a warm hearth and succulent homemade beef pie, not to mention the attentions of a woman, something he had missed very much since his last divorce.

It seemed natural that, after a suitably appropriate time, Timothy should propose marriage to Amelia.

"After all…" He smiled at her benignly. "It does seem silly to run two homes when we spend so much of our time together."

Amelia Smith had no hesitation in accepting. She had been gratified from the start to learn that Timothy shared her love of silence and seemed completely content without television. She had mentioned in passing that she had a radio in the kitchen and occasionally it was turned on to obtain the news or weather and on one occasion Amelia had found herself listening, without panic, to a play. But the episode had unnerved her and had not been repeated, the radio remaining silent for several weeks after that.

Timothy seemed to have no inclination for entertainment, although he did sometimes mention radio programmes in a rather hesitant way, his knowledge in that area seeming quite extensive. But, when she protested, he didn't pursue the matter and Amelia was quite sure their life together would be harmonious.

She explained very carefully one evening, when the spring sunshine shone through the cottage windows and the birds chirped merrily in the trees outside, her love of solitude. It had been difficult at first, talking about her childhood, but Timothy had put a comforting arm around her shoulders and the words had poured out.

She confessed she had shared a tiny bedroom with two older sisters, her brothers equally cramped together in the next room. Early mornings were a cacophony of radio alarms; announcers vying for dominance, her father's voice roaring louder than all put together, the discordant tumult of babble resounding throughout the terraced house. She tried to explain the fear that made her cower beneath the blankets, shaking, until banging doors heralded departures and an uneasy silence settled in the turbulent atmosphere. Then she would scuttle timidly about the rooms and sneak off to school. Even now a passing car radio could invoke that terrified fear. Her childhood was dominated by her passionate longing for quiet, her nature being alien to the life she had been born to, her family abhorrent to her gentle soul.

To the young Amelia quietude was a distant dream. Quiet was just a word in the dictionary. Amelia studied the dictionary. She studied her schoolbooks, she found escape in novels. She was different. Her mother watched her, bemused. Her father frowned at her. A cuckoo in the nest; he found her quiet intelligence uncomfortable.

When the rent collector called, her father glared at him. A clever man, the rent collector. Had his wife been unfaithful? It was one explanation for this misfit in his house. Then he looked at his blousy, unkempt wife with her gin bottle alongside the teapot and disclaimed that idea. When would she find the time, or space? No, Amelia was incomprehensible. He dismissed her presence with a scowl and vent his confused anger on his wife.

When Amelia's brothers left school and became unemployed, or some of them, self-employed – two of the self-employed ending up in prison which eased the load in the little house – and Amelia's sisters moved into terraced houses up the street with their partner's families, Amelia slunk from her home and headed for the suburbs. If her family noticed her disappearance, it was with relief.

She went into catering. As a waitress she could work evenings. No radio alarms for her. Her mornings were peaceful and undisturbed. She reached out and sucked in the tranquillity.

She progressed to a cottage in the country and the quiet was heaven. She refused to have a television. She opened the windows to the sound of birds, she awoke in the mornings naturally, no raucous cacophonies for her; in fact, she became obsessive about her silence.

Then, maturing in years, she realised she was lonely. It was a shock to discover this fact and, after all the years of self-interest, she found it unnerving. But the thought of sharing her solitude persisted. Enquiring casually at the local Post Office she discovered the presence of other lonely people, in the Singles Club. It turned out to be rather an adventure. Despite her misgivings and first failed marriage to Charlie, which had been easily remedied, she persevered. Now there was Timothy.

At the end of her narrative Timothy patted her arm in the most loving fashion and wiped her tears, assuring her she had no need to worry. He would take care of her for the rest of her days, her happiness being of paramount importance to him and her love of silence utterly respected.

Amelia sighed. If only Charlie had reacted in the same way. A few days later, encouraged into further confession, she explained very carefully to Timothy the faults that her first husband had possessed. Once confidence had been established she felt happier in relaying such facts and, as she had no intention of being unhappily married again, she hoped Timothy would take heed of her words. Not that she thought for a moment that Timothy would annoy her as Charlie had done, but one had to be sure.

"It was Charlie's work, you see," she confided. "I could never accept what he did. It was such an upsetting occupation. I'm sure there were many people who gave a sigh of relief when it was announced he had suffered a heart attack. Not that I ever criticised of course." She sighed sadly. "But it was so hard to bear. I think, had he lived, I would have left him eventually; my heart couldn't have stood the aggravation much longer. As it was…" She raised her eyes heavenward in silent thanks.

Being a withdrawn person herself she had not been upset by the fact that Timothy was rather evasive about his occupation. For the sake of peace, Amelia felt quite sure that the information would be given to her if it were necessary and she accepted his vague description that he did 'something in advertising'. She was quite happy not to know further details and had no intention of going with him to the city, being content to wait in her cottage for his return each evening. He certainly appeared to have no financial problems and vacated the house every morning in his city suit, returned promptly at six in the evening.

A few days before the wedding Amelia ventured to question

him, having been embarrassed in the Post Office by well-meaning villagers who were curious about Timothy. "It's just that I'm interested in what you do all day, Timothy. Obviously I know you have a most acceptable job…"

"I promise I will never upset you, dearest." Timothy's words comforted her. "After all you suffered with Charlie's career, I don't want to bore you with details of my work. Suffice it to say it is very respectable, and I am a well-known person in the city. Perhaps one day…"

Amelia had to be content with this and concentrated on her forthcoming nuptials.

The first shock of anxiety rose in Amelia's mind one day when she had been shopping. So far their union had surpassed all her expectations and the days had merged into weeks with Amelia thanking her lucky stars for this second chance of happiness.

When she returned this particular Saturday, Timothy had gone out. Taking her coat into the bedroom she stopped, rooted to the spot, her eyes widening at the contraption that ill-graced the bedside table. A radio alarm! Timothy had mentioned on several occasions that he was having difficulty in waking in the mornings and Amelia knew how punctual he liked to be, but a radio alarm!

A radio in the mornings, disturbing her silence, was unacceptable. She had thought Timothy understood this, understood her need for perfect peace, quiet at all costs. He'd always been so careful not to arouse her when he'd slipped out of bed to go to work, touching her brow with a light kiss as he'd crept from the room.

Now it looked as if the tranquillity of her slumbers was to be disturbed, again! Hadn't she suffered enough with Charlie? Didn't Timothy realise this? Her confidence shivered and shattered as she glared at the alien monstrosity by her bed. Panic curled around her heart and frolicked in her stomach. What on earth was she to do? She took shelter in her usual response to fear, speechlessness.

When they went to bed that night she didn't mention the clock and she turned from Timothy, in the hope of blotting the squatting threat from her sight. Memories from her childhood invaded her mind and she shivered beneath the blankets, fear resounding from the dregs of her being. Not again! It was intolerable.

The next morning a dazed Amelia scrambled through a nightmare of fog to hear an unfamiliar voice explaining how to eliminate carrot fly. Carrot fly? Flustered, she raised herself on an elbow and stared at Timothy, appalled.

"Timothy…" Her voice croaked to a stop. "What on earth…?"

"Sorry, my dear, I was hoping it wouldn't disturb you. You normally sleep so soundly." He smiled absently as he turned his ear to the details of making garden compost.

Amelia refused to believe she was awake. It was a dream she was experiencing; yes, she was still asleep. She sank back on the pillows as Timothy turned and switched off the radio. Horrified, she realised this was no dream.

"Very interesting." He was grinning broadly and Amelia wondered if he'd lost his senses in the night.

"Interesting?" she squeaked.

"Yes. Growing your own vegetables. A fascinating subject."

Timothy had never expressed an interest in vegetables before and Amelia felt he could have divulged this information at a better time.

"But we haven't got a garden!" She could feel the palpitations beginning deep in her chest.

"I know, more's the pity." Timothy leapt from the bed. "Still, perhaps one day… In the meantime I shall enjoy listening to the programme. It's only on for a quarter of an hour, wakes me up nicely. Now my dear…" He kissed Amelia's stunned face. "You go back to sleep and I'll bring you a nice cup of tea."

After Timothy left, totally oblivious of her churning feelings, she tried to relax. It was impossible. Vegetables, first thing in the morning, and compost, and all so noisily!

Amelia felt extremely disturbed for the rest of the day. She began to have doubts about the wisdom of her marriage. Had Timothy listened to anything she had said, had he understood her needs at all?

After three mornings of potatoes, greenfly and root rot, she knew something would have to be done. She couldn't understand why Timothy found the whole situation so hilarious every evening, when she broached the subject of getting rid of the radio.

"Certainly not, my dear," he chuckled. "This is my little surprise."

"Surprise?" she replied faintly.

"Yes." He laughed and pinched her chin. "And you still haven't guessed, have you?"

He went into the kitchen chortling to himself.

"Guessed?" Amelia sank onto the sofa completely nonplussed. "Guessed what?"

Timothy returned with a glass and pressed it into her trembling hand as he sat beside her.

"Well, my dear, now we've been together for a while and have proved how happy we can be, I thought it was about time you knew."

"Knew?" Amelia took a large gulp of whisky and nearly choked.

"Yes." Timothy took her free hand and patted her on the back. "I know how you felt about Charlie's occupation, how irritated you were by his profession. I understand the horrors of your childhood, but that was all a long time ago and can hardly have any bearing on our present happiness. That's why I've waited until now to impart the nature of my work."

"The nature of your work?" Amelia sipped again, a sinking feeling in her stomach telling her she was not going to like what she was to hear.

"Yes." Timothy grinned. "The vegetable programme. I broadcast it!"

Amelia gaped and promptly fainted across the cushions. Timothy removed the empty glass from her hand and fanned her pale cheeks. As she recovered he tried explaining. "I knew you'd be surprised, but surely it's not that bad. After all, you can hardly compare my sensible talk with Charlie's…"

He trailed off at the look of pure hatred on his wife's face.

★

Amelia Townsend, widow, rejoined the Singles Club.

"We're so sorry to hear about Timothy's heart attack," the members consoled her soothingly. "So soon after your marriage too."

Amelia accepted their condolences and affected a sad look. She was sad. She had thought Timothy was different, but a radio announcer, just like her Charlie! Charlie had never understood, either, her obsession with silence, particularly in the mornings.

True, Charlie had wakened her earlier, his talk on natural medicines not as popular as Timothy's on vegetables and pest control. If only men weren't so keen to hear their own voices!

"You'll talk yourself into the grave," her mother used to tell her father. Amelia always remembered that saying. It was the only truth her mother ever uttered.

She had learnt a lot from Charlie's talks, even practising the recipes herself, and so far they had been very effective. Charlie'd had his uses, in the end. She knew how healing herbs and flowers could be, or how lethal, if one made the tiniest mistake in preparation. Add to that, the knowledge she had gleaned, albeit unwillingly, from Timothy's advice on pest control, and she now felt completely equipped to control her life admirably.

"Practise makes perfect," she murmured as she surveyed the newcomers to the Singles Club. She turned brightly as a soft touch on her arm swung her towards a pink-faced gentlemen.

"Amelia, I'd like you to meet William. He's new to the Club, recently divorced."

Amelia smiled hopefully into gentle blue eyes.

"Hello, William. Tell me, have you ever considered broadcasting on the radio?"

release dot com

To: alphonse smith@helpmates.co.uk
Re: Possible liaison
14 August – 10.00

Dear Alphonse

I can call you Alphonse, can't I? Mr Smith seems rather sinister somehow. Although we've never met, I feel I know you well. When I read your biography on the Net, I formed a picture of you in my mind. I could be wrong, of course, I usually am. I'm rather nervous, never having approached a stranger in this way before.

Anyway, I'd better introduce myself. My name's Miranda and I've been married to Kurt for ten years. My husband is usually away; his business takes him all over the country. We moved to this isolated cottage a few years ago and I find I'm often lonely.

If you're open to offers and would like details of my proposition, please reply – before Saturday if you can. On Saturday Kurt comes home.

Miranda

14 August – 13.00

Dear Alphonse

Isn't e-mail amazing? I just popped out for some fresh air, it's a glorious day, and when I returned, your answer was waiting. Wonderful. Thank you so much for taking an interest.

This is Kurt's PC, but I decided that practising on the computer was a good way to pass the time. I found out how to 'surf the Net' and then I found your website, 'Helpmates'. It sounded rather interesting, so much more so than 'Playmates' or 'Friends', and I thought I'd check out the register. And there you were. You sound just what I'm looking for, if you're willing of course.

Certainly I'll tell you more about myself. I do get so bored here on my own, with no job to alleviate the tediousness. I had a career once, in banking. For the first time in my life I felt useful. I love figures, so logical, and the manager seemed to think I had an aptitude for the work. This made me feel good, something I hadn't felt before.

Then Kurt came along. I enjoyed his masterful ways; he made me feel protected and loved. I always longed to be wanted and looked after. Kurt walked into my life and made me feel wonderfully safe, so I married him. I didn't realise I'd misunderstood his attitude. Kurt's an old fashioned man; the woman's place is in the home and all that, which is fine, if there are children. Anyway, enough about me. Where do we go from here?

Miranda

15 August – 09.00

Dear Alphonse

Fancy you being in Security. Kurt's in Security too. Fascinating isn't it, what the word 'security' means in different businesses, so unlike the dictionary definition. I'm sure you're a true professional, just like Kurt.

Obviously I don't expect references; some things have to be taken on trust, don't they? No, I don't get out a lot, not on my own. The last time Kurt was home I had a nasty fall and broke my ankle, so hobbling around here is about all I can manage at the moment. Kurt says I'm accident-prone; at least that's what he tells his friends. I do seem to sustain injuries regularly; but I'm sure you don't want to hear about my woes. Actually, I feel quite cheerful at the moment; it's planning positively for the future, turning my day-dream into reality. Uplifting stuff, eh?

I'm enjoying this. What happens next?

Miranda

★

15 August – 14.00

Dear Alphonse

Yes, of course I'll forward details of my plan. I'll send an attachment. I've already looked up how to do that in 'Help'.

And yes, I have followed all your instructions (thanks for detailing the process so explicitly). The files are deleted and I've emptied the Recycle Bin. There's no trace of your e-mails left. I'll continue to erase any communication between us – obviously I don't want Kurt finding any clue to the fact that I've been on his computer at all. I need to protect myself from repercussions. I realised that last weekend when one of Kurt's clients upset him; he showed me a picture of those repercussions. I had asked him for a divorce at the time; but a divorce is not the answer. I hope you are.

However, I digress. Time is suddenly flying by and I'm rather anxious. I'll leave all the arrangements to you, being the professional.

I look forward to hearing from you.

Miranda

★

16 August – 08.00

Hi Alphonse

Thank you for the prompt reply and for the attachment (I had a bit of hassle with that, but it's arrived). I accept your terms for our agreement. My husband will be funding my indulgence, rather ironic I think. I shall add you to his client list. I spent a few hours yesterday familiarising myself with his records. He certainly has a full book. The investigation proved depressing. I wish Kurt could have been in a more mundane job, but that wouldn't have suited his nature at all.

Don't worry; I have no intention of reneging on our deal. I'm so excited that I haven't room for guilt. That might come later. I do hope not. I'm sure a reminder of my desperate unhappiness will quell any unpleasant niggles in that direction. To convince you I intend to go through with this, I'll send a cheque as requested (thanks for the PO Box number) for half the amount now and, provided I am fully satisfied with your performance, the remainder will follow in due course.

Yours in anticipation

Miranda

16 August – 16.00

Alphonse

You sound very professional. I'm impressed! Yes, Kurt is working in London at the moment; he's staying at the Railway Hotel, which overlooks the Thames I believe. Is this your home area? What a coincidence if it is, it makes this subterfuge even more exciting. Obviously he'd be horrified if he found out about our liaison, but with you being in Security I know you understand confidentiality.

Of course I'll send you a photo. I'll put it in the post with the cheque tonight. It was taken a while ago but it's a good likeness.

Miranda

★

19 August – 14.00

Alphonse

I can't really believe your last e-mail. I had to re-read it several times until the truth sank in. Our little game is over. Thank you so much for everything you've done. You're fantastic, worth every penny. Even though our acquaintance has been short, it has changed my life dramatically. I still can't believe my scheme worked. But it has.

The police confirmed the fact earlier this morning. They were very sympathetic. My shock at their news was genuine. 'A terrible accident,' they said. 'He fell from the balcony of his hotel into the Thames.' He'd been drinking of course. 'A tragic accident,' they stressed. Amazing.

I've put a final cheque in the post and I've added the amount requested to cover your expenses.

Yours in appreciation

Miranda

2 September – 11.00

Mr Smith
I am bitterly disappointed to receive another e-mail from you. We agreed terms when we first corresponded and I've kept my side of the bargain. To demand further payment is just not acceptable.

I shall be moving shortly. Since Kurt's death I've made various arrangements to start a new life. Fortunately my husband's business was very profitable. Kurt was good at his job if nothing else. He had, I grant you, a vicious temper, which was probably a necessary tool to his trade, but never once did he arouse suspicion. I have notified his clients of his demise and no doubt heartfelt whoops of joy are being echoed across the country. I have also told them that I do not intend to pursue any outstanding debts.

In view of my compassion to these unfortunate people, I do find it extremely offensive that you intend to pursue me for a debt I do not owe. Please do not attempt to emulate Kurt. Blackmail, Mr Smith, is a very ugly business and I would advise you against it. Each to his own I say and I suggest you pursue your chosen career, for which you are perfectly suited, rather than attempt to dabble in extortion.

M.

★

3 September – 6.00

Mr Smith
I am about to format my hard disk and disconnect my telephone. I refuse to be intimidated by your threats. This, Mr Smith, is my final communication.

M.

To: demetrius smith@helpmates.co.uk
Re: Possible liaison
3 September – 6.15

Dear Demetrius

I can call you Demetrius, can't I? Mr Smith seems rather sinister somehow. I'm wondering if you can help me with a little problem I have. I am shortly catching a flight for Spain (I'll contact you when I arrive) and I'm looking forward to a future free from stress. If you e-mail me a contact address by return, I will send you a cheque, which will, I hope, cover initial expenses for the removal of an unnecessary encumbrance that is making my life rather unpleasant. You should be familiar with him. His name is Alphonse Smith.

Miss M.

Natural Potential

The day that Jake had all his teeth removed proved to be a catalyst to a startling upsurge in his fortune. Not that he realised that at the time. All he felt at the moment of reviving from the anaesthetic was pain. His mouth felt worse than from any meeting with angry fists, and he'd had many of those in his life. No, this pain was definitely different and he repeatedly assured the nurse of that fact until he was administered with painkillers.

They allowed him home, if the dingy bed-sit on the top floor of the crumbling building in the back streets of the city could be called that; allowed him home in his misery despite the fact that he was adamant that there was no one to care for him.

"Now Mr Malone…" The nurse was chiding him in the same tone of voice she reserved for the children's ward. "You've only had your teeth out. We've given you plenty of painkillers. Just rest and sip some warm soup. Tomorrow you'll feel differently and we'll see you then to check your gums."

So home he had to go, in a taxi he could ill-afford.

The next day he didn't feel differently. The ache in his head, the pain in his gums and the general feeling of sickness all encouraged the thought that life wasn't worth living. He'd wondered about this fact before, but never as vehemently as he did that morning when he managed to lever his protesting body to the bathroom and unexpectedly faced himself in the mirror.

"My God!" He clutched the side of the washbasin and slowly

his eyes assimilated his face. Only it didn't look like his face. His lips wobbled like a too-big rubber band stuck to the hole that was his mouth. His skin hung from his forehead like over-kneaded plasticine, drooping across his eyes and slithering down his cheeks to hang in two great droplets either side of his chin. Even his cheekbones seem to have surrendered to the avalanche of skin and disappeared beneath the blubber.

"My God!" he repeated, unable to form any coherent thoughts. "Who are you?"

He hailed another taxi and scurried into the hospital for his check-up swathed in a large scarf and woolly hat. The thought of recognition on the way and the necessity for explanation left him quaking. Not that anyone would recognise him, he predicted gloomily. The monster from the slime had better features than his at the moment.

"No one will know me," he told the doctor angrily. "I look horrendous!"

The doctor was irreverently cheerful. "It's only for a little while. The face will adjust and then, of course, you'll have your new teeth."

Jake glared at him and slunk home.

He didn't want new teeth. He'd been very proud of his old ones, until the rotting disease had taken hold. And, he admitted, just lately he hadn't been taking care of them as he should. He blamed the last little disaster that had proved he was getting past it. A mistake here, a slip there and his face had ended up as a punch ball. Several of his teeth had been loosened and some broken. What with that and the doctor informing him that most of the rest of his teeth were rotting, he agreed to have them removed.

"A much better idea altogether, one big pain instead of prolonged misery." The doctor was unshakably cheerful. In no fit state to argue, defeated, Jake had signed his teeth away, reflecting dejectedly on his deteriorating looks.

Handsome, he'd been called, and charming. He was only fifty and he'd hoped to have a few more working years ahead of him. He was broke and needed to work. There had been a lot of gloomy moments like this in his life, but he'd always bounced back. He'd smiled and charmed and there you'd go; he'd be in the money again. A fat chance of that now, looking like this, he moaned to himself. Who's going to take any notice of me, looking like this?

In his bathroom he took the mirror from the wall and slid it behind the towel. Not that it made him feel any better but at least he wouldn't have the disgusting reminder every time he washed. For the next few days he sat in muttering misery living off packet soup.

As the pain eased his optimistic spirit played with ideas and gradually one fact kept flitting through his mind until it lodged in his consciousness and became inspiration. *No one will recognise me like this*. Of course they wouldn't! This offered possibilities. Always one to grasp opportunities Jake stood up, rescued the mirror and stared at himself. "No one will recognise me like this," he repeated joyously and, stretching himself on the sofa, he allowed his imagination to roam.

It was three weeks until he could have his new teeth fitted. One of those weeks had already been wasted in useless self-pity, but there were two weeks left. Two weeks in which to take advantage of his changed appearance. Fate had not deserted him after all; on the contrary, fate had presented him with a glorious opportunity. All it needed was a little planning and he was back in business; and there was one piece of unfinished business that would bring him the retirement he had fantasised about with Gloria.

The thought of Gloria rekindled familiar nostalgia that welled up inside him. They had dreamed so many wonderful plans, working hard together on their culmination. Gloria. He sighed as he remembered their first meeting. He'd been brandishing a gun at the time, not a real one of course, but a very lifelike replica. He was rather proud of his homemade creation; it had served its purpose on more than one occasion.

As usual, Jake had been down on his luck. His previous expedition into someone else's business had left him with sore ribs and little else. He was broke. Desperate action was called for. He searched out his black gun, donned his poacher coat and, pulling a balaclava over his head, he rushed into the post office brandishing the firearm and shouting suitably ferociously. As soon as his eyes met Gloria's, his heart sank. Sparkling blue eyes bored like gimlets through his woolly headgear and pierced his defences. She was beautiful and she was angry.

"Put that stupid thing away!" Hands on the counter, she leaned over and held his eyes with her own. "Do you hear me?"

Jake was confounded. Never before had anyone argued with his gun. He wondered if he was losing his touch. Perhaps he was getting too old for this sort of caper. It was time he left it to the youngsters.

"Just give me the money," he pleaded but she shook her head. She was a determined woman; he was to find that out later, to his cost.

"Not on your life." She folded her arms, her eyes never leaving his. "Put that down and stop being so silly."

Silly was one thing he'd never been called, a lot of other names over the years but silly, never. He stared at Gloria; flame-red hair framed sharply accentuated features and her luscious lips were pursed tightly. Thick lashes framed the blueness of her eyes that now shot shards of ice to his very soul. His stomach gurgled and his heart lurched. He was defeated.

What on earth could he do? With a sigh of resignation he put the toy in his pocket and slouched out. He pulled the balaclava from his head and, as the alarm sounded, he ran. Up the alley, across the back road and there was a nice little café, looking safe and comforting. He counted the change in his pocket and ordered a mug of tea. He was hungry but he didn't have enough money to buy food. He sat at one of the pretty tables and studied the ketchup pot gloomily.

Gloria had shaken his confidence; there was no doubt about it. He didn't feel he could try that trick again. Perhaps the supermarket for something slipped into his pockets? But they all had surveillance cameras and he'd probably get caught. Everything was so complicated these days. He longed for the years of his youth when he used to saunter into a shop, choose what he wanted and walk out. No cameras, no guards, all nice and simple. Perhaps he ought to have trained for a respectable job when he left school; but it was too late now.

His tea was slowly cooling, but he wanted to make it last. It was warm in the café and his present digs were pretty miserable. He almost choked when the door opened and in walked Gloria. His heart started to thump but even in his panic he registered what a lovely girl she was, just the type he would normally go for. She ordered tea and turned around. Her eyes met his and in that second he betrayed himself. She recognised him. For a moment she stood still and then she headed for his table, sitting opposite him.

"Not your day is it?" she remarked as she sipped her drink.

Jake glared at her. "Well?" He attempted bravado but the wobble in his voice exposed him. "Well, what are you going to do about it?"

"I don't know yet." She continued to watch him, her eyes travelling over his face and as far down his body as she could see. "Perhaps you'd like to tell me why you tried to scare me witless."

"I needed the money."

"Obviously." She waited.

"I'm broke." He was sounding sorry for himself. "I don't know how else to get money."

"Your disguise wasn't very original."

"I've others," he told her eagerly, sensing an unusual tolerance. "Usually I'm pretty good. I've never got caught, but this morning I was desperate."

She nodded and gazed at him reflectively. "You hungry?" He nodded. She ordered two breakfasts. He couldn't believe his luck and knew that payback time would come. But for now he feasted on his sausage and bacon, too ravenous to be cautious.

Thinking back now Jake had to smile. They had enjoyed some wonderful times together. He never understood what made Gloria pitch her lot in with him. He was attractive to women, he knew that, but he was broke and his income was unreliable.

"Why?" he asked her, as they lay supine in bed.

She traced the outline of his face with her finger and smiled. "You had potential."

He liked that.

"You just needed some managing. Besides," she kissed him slowly, "I fancied your eyes. I like desperate eyes."

He was content.

Gloria persuaded him to start a business. They rented a shop in the city centre and set up a fancy dress outlet. They called it 'Hire a Fantasy'. It appealed to him. Fancy dress parties were all the rage and, as the business went well, they expanded into tricks and disguises, all of which he tested to make sure they were viable.

Their wealth grew. The official business flourished and the nest egg under the shop floor expanded. One brown envelope became two and then three and Jake looked forward to the comfort of early retirement; in Spain, they agreed. Gloria ran the shop and he provided the nest egg. They had an amazing partnership and, besides that, he actually loved her. Their double bed was a bonus.

Life was perfect, until Terry came on the scene. Terry was horribly handsome; not only was he handsome, but he could have wheedled his way into a locked safe. One day he walked into the shop and the next night, it seemed to Jake, Terry was in his bed. Jake was out, a suitcase in one hand, a cheque in the other, dented with Terry's indelible scrawl. It happened so quickly Jake was flummoxed, so flummoxed he forgot the nest egg. The nest egg was left behind; temporarily, he reminded himself later.

When he regained his senses and asked Gloria for a share, she refused. He slammed down the phone in outrage. His nest egg! But she was a determined woman and wouldn't budge. He couldn't have the nest egg. He wondered if she had mentioned it to Terry and he began plotting.

He tried many schemes to get his hands on that money. Bribery, pathetic pleading, burglary; all failed. Terry was too astute for him and Gloria was too tough. The money stayed under the floorboards. He could hardly take Gloria to court for the unofficial bounty and she knew that. The money from the cheque lasted him for a while but, as money was inclined to do when it wasn't topped up, it ran out, as did his imagination.

So here he was, broke and toothless and, as he examined his appearance once more in the mirror, he wondered if, at last, his chance had come. Would Terry see through this disguise? He could feel his potential flourishing again and he knew he had to act quickly. It was time to try for his nest egg once more. The last time he had walked by 'Hire a Fantasy' he had noticed a *For Sale* sign. That could only mean one thing. Gloria and Terry were high-tailing it out of the country, pursuing his dreams, with his nest egg.

He waited impatiently until the day before his false teeth were due to invade his mouth. He donned his poacher coat, now somewhat frayed around the edges, and sauntered through the streets. Outside the shop his nerve almost failed him. Slouch, he muttered, slouch and shuffle, shuffle and slouch. He could see Terry posing arrogantly behind the counter and, taking a deep breath, he pushed open the door.

"Can I help you, sir?"

Sir, Terry was calling him sir!

Jake sucked his flabby lips into his mouth. Now was not the time to smile. "I'm looking for an outfit for my niece." His voice was sloppy.

"Of course, have a browse." Terry smiled smugly and gestured towards the showroom.

Jake turned slowly away; shuffle, slouch. He hardly breathed; so far so good, unbelievable. This was one disguise Gloria hadn't got in her shop, and Terry hadn't recognised him. He shuffled between the rows of costumes. No one else was around and there was no sign of Gloria. In the back corner of the room he saw the chair that guarded the nest egg. He moved quickly. From his pocket he pulled a slim knife and, slipping it between the floorboards, he prised one up. He paused and listened. He heard the sound of Terry's voice in conversation, which meant that, at any moment, someone could walk in.

Jake felt the sweat break out on his body. After waiting for so long he couldn't be defeated now. His hand trembled as it slipped into the darkness and then he touched a packet. One, two and the third, he levered into his pockets. That was the lot. He slipped the board back into place and pushed the chair gently to its protecting position.

The door opened and Terry was silhouetted in the doorway, with Gloria. Jake held up a monkey outfit he had hastily grabbed, twirled it around and set it back on the rail. Nonchalantly he passed by them.

"I'll send her in," he mumbled as he reached the door.

"Thanks, old chap." Terry's voice was condescending. Then the bell clanged and the door shut after him. He was in the street. He had done it, right in the face of Gloria and Terry and they hadn't recognised him.

His coat hung weightily low on the one side as he shuffled away. He slouched gleefully along trying to keep his pace slow. It was difficult. When he reached his room he dared a glance in the packets. It was all there. All his hard earned money. With any luck Gloria wouldn't check the hidey-hole for a while and even then she couldn't report the theft, because officially the nest egg didn't exist!

The next day saw him bright and early at the dentist. His suitcase waited in reception, his new coat folded neatly over it.

The dentist noted his smart suit. "Going away?"

"Just a little holiday." Jake gaped in the semblance of a grin and relaxed in the chair.

His disguise now eradicated, Jake sat on the plane listening to the engines revving. He settled comfortably in his seat and closed his eyes.

'Barcelona, here I come!' In his mind's eye he could see the Spanish city bathed in sunshine and full of promise. His pristine teeth glowed in the darkness of his mouth and he gave a sigh of satisfaction. The potential that Gloria had recognised in him had been realised at last.

His only regret was that Gloria wasn't with him to share the fulfilment of their dreams. But that was hardly *his* fault, was it?

Dream Lover

He was the most gorgeous man at the party and Donna recognised him immediately. Their eyes met across the swaying heads and she knew by his smile that he remembered her too. He pushed his way through the crowd and Donna felt anticipation quicken her heartbeat.

"Hello." He took her hand in his and raised it to his lips and she felt his warm breath sweep to the tips of her fingers. "I knew we'd meet again."

Donna smiled and nodded, feeling slightly uncomfortable. No one could forget a man like this, the proverbial tall, dark and handsome, with a smile that would melt the thickest iceberg. But his name? How could she possibly forget his name?

As she said to her flat-mate, Susie, the next morning, "I felt mortified, absolutely mortified! I don't think he realised... But not to remember his name!"

"Unlike you, old thing." Susie laughed. "Scatterbrained you may be, but as far as men are concerned..." She shook her head. "Where did you meet him?"

Donna frowned. "That's something else." She paused. "I can't remember that either!"

Susie looked startled.

★

Donna had spent the whole evening pondering that question. His friend, Henry, supplied her with a name…

"May I introduce Henry?" Donna had hardly noticed the man by his side. Shorter and plain with springing brown curls, he beamed delightedly at Donna.

"Ah, Donna, yes, of course." He shook her hand energetically. "I thought for a moment Stephen was going to keep you all to himself and not introduce us!"

'Stephen.' Donna smiled politely at Henry and glanced sideways at his companion.

Perhaps they'd never been introduced? Perhaps she'd seen him on a bus, in the supermarket? Unless, of course, he had a wife to do the shopping!

They chatted sociably. Their mutual knowledge of the hostess, Donna's work in a lawyer's office, the weather, holidays; and all through the conversation Donna placed him in situations in her imagination.

He knew her name. It was a puzzle. Could he possibly be a client?

How on earth could he have passed through her life, however briefly, without leaving a lasting and vividly detailed memory?

In the end Donna gave up worrying, aware of the amusement in his dark eyes. It was almost as if he knew her thoughts and was enjoying her dilemma. She decided to relax in the pleasure of his company and, when he asked her to dance, she slipped willingly into his arms.

Perhaps, when she was alone and had time to think, she would recall their previous encounter. At that moment the past seemed irrelevant.

It was an amazing evening. Stephen hardly left her side, neither did Henry but, as Henry was an amusing and lively companion, she found herself enjoying the party. Stephen offered little conversation but made his presence known with a touch on her arm, a gentle laugh and the occasional whispered remark.

They shared a taxi, the three of them, so there was no time for Donna to be alone with Stephen. The taxi waited, engine running, as he walked her to the door.

"I'll phone you tomorrow."

She nodded and, glowing with happiness, ran up the stairs to the flat. She heard the taxi pull away and it wasn't until she had locked the door and hung up her coat that she remembered that she hadn't given him her telephone number.

She consoled herself with the thought that he knew where she lived and crept quietly into bed. Susie was already asleep.

"What does he do?" Susie continued now, her curiosity aroused.

"I don't know." Donna realised that Stephen has said very little about himself. "Henry mentioned that he and Stephen shared a house down by the river."

"Expensive part of town!" Susie mused. "He must have a good income to own one of those."

Donna nodded, a slight frown on her brow.

"Well..." Susie got up and went to refill the kettle. "It strikes me you've fallen in love with a man you know nothing about! Are you sure you *have* met him before?"

"Of course!" Donna was certain. "Besides, he knew my name, he even seemed to know where I live."

"Perhaps he's a stalker," Susie said cheerfully. "Been following you about and you've seen him in a crowd behind you."

Donna stared at her in horror. "Oh, never!"

Susie laughed. "Of course not, silly. It all seems a bit vague that's all. Besides, if his intentions had been dishonorable he wouldn't have carted Henry along, would he?"

"No, I suppose not." Donna sounded relieved. "And Henry was such a nice man, fun."

"And Stephen?" Susie glanced at her as she placed mugs on the table.

"Just... gorgeous!"

Donna's eyes were dreamy, but the shrill ring of the telephone interrupted her thoughts.

"For you!" Susie waved the receiver in the air and mouthed, 'It's him!'

Donna grabbed the phone and silently waved Susie away.

"Hello, Donna."

His rich voice dispelled any lingering doubts in Donna's mind.

"It's such a lovely day, I wondered if you'd like to come for a walk this afternoon? We could go to the park. We've so much to talk about."

She didn't hesitate. Replacing the receiver she rushed to the bedroom.

Donna was waiting as the taxi drew up and she felt her heart quicken as she almost fell into the seat beside him, his warmth enveloping her and his eyes smiling into hers. She was relieved to see there was no sign of Henry.

It was a magical afternoon, ending with a wonderful meal and, as he walked her home through the dark streets, she felt as if she had known him forever.

She had talked too much, as usual, but he was such a good listener, and it wasn't until she lay in bed fingering her lips still sensitive from his kiss, that she realised she still knew very little about him.

'Next time,' she resolved, as she turned over and fell into a deep sleep, 'next time I shall do the listening.'

The spring days lengthened into summer and Donna knew she loved Stephen, a love deeper than any she had ever experienced before.

She was certain Stephen felt the same way.

Sometimes she would turn unexpectedly and catch him looking at her with an expression of such brooding intensity that she found it slightly disquieting.

He could be disturbingly arrogant and Donna began to notice that he rarely asked her when or where they should go but, as she had always been disorganised, his dominance was welcome and she enjoyed whatever he planned.

"Masterful, that's what he is," she told Susie.

Susie had her doubts.

"Have you ever said no to any of his plans?" she asked.

"Why should I?" Donna was surprised. "He never suggests

anything I don't agree with. I'm happy being with him and that's all that matters."

"Try disagreeing with him sometime," Susie answered, but Donna shook her head.

"I don't need to," she replied stubbornly.

Susie looked worried, but shrugged and turned away.

Sometimes Henry accompanied them on their outings. Donna always enjoyed his company. His sense of fun matched hers and their ridiculous antics amused Stephen, sometimes.

Occasionally Donna caught Stephen watching them speculatively, separating himself from them, his mouth hard.

Then Donna would leave Henry and slip her arm through Stephen's, waiting, leaning against his side, anxious, until she felt the tension ease from his body and saw the smile back in his eyes as he gazed at her.

It was on one of the shortest nights of the year that Donna had the dream. As always, when she had been out with Stephen, she slept immediately. It was twilight when she went to sleep and, for the first time, her dreams were disturbing.

She was running, panting and exhausted, through thick woods. Spiked brambles caught her long skirts, the heavy brocade hampering her flight as she tried to beat a path through the dense undergrowth. The hem of her petticoat was muddied and torn, and her shawl, tied roughly around her waist slipped from her shoulders.

In her arms a child cried, clinging to her bodice, scarcely protected from the whipping branches by the shawl, which she hurriedly secured to keep the child against her breast.

Ahead of her a man tried futilely to break a path for her to follow. His slender stick was mocked as bent briars sprang viciously upright behind him.

"Hurry, Henry, hurry!" Her voice was urgent and fear filled her heart as the sound of horse's hooves thundered nearer.

And then the undergrowth parted, miraculously, into a clearing. Soft grass beneath warm sun, birds sang. She took a rasping breath and steadied herself, gathering her skirts as her steps quickened.

Suddenly she stopped. It was too late. The pursuer swung from his horse and confronted her, eyes blazing.

"Give me my son!"

She shrank from his hatred and stepped back, but with one cruel wrench her shawl lay torn on the grass. The child whimpered as strong arms pulled him from her grasp and nestled him away from her.

He stared at her silently, eyes black with emotion as she sank to her knees, sobbing.

"Stephen." She raised her head, reaching hands towards him beseechingly. "Stephen, forgive me!"

He shook his head and, holding the boy with one arm, he circled his horse.

"I shall come back for you one day, never doubt it!" His eyes pierced icicles into hers, and she knew it was a promise he would keep. She was filled with dread.

"Henry…" He stared at the man who stood silently on the edge of the glade and she saw the anguish on their faces. "Take her, she's yours."

The horse spun and was gone, the sound of hooves dying with the cries of the child.

What had she done? Harsh sobs wracked her body but when she screamed for Henry, he too had gone.

"Donna, Donna!" Susie was shaking her shoulders and she gasped as she opened her eyes. Tears were streaming down her face.

"Donna, what is it?" Susie looked scared.

"A dream, just a dream!" Donna smiled shakily. "A terrible nightmare."

"It must have been!" Susie relaxed. "Try and go back to sleep!"

Donna lay on the damp pillow and felt that she never wanted to sleep again.

The dream had been so vivid, so real. Stephen and Henry, and the child, a son; hers and Stephen's? She shuddered.

She still felt the fear, the terror.

Henry had offered her escape, escape for her and her son, from Stephen. From Stephen – why?

But it had been useless. There was no escape from Stephen. She felt the hopelessness mingle with the fear within her. It was all so clear in her mind, in precise detail.

'I shall come back for you, never doubt it.'

He had promised.

As she lay watching the dawn filter through her curtains she was filled with foreboding.

It seemed a long time until the alarm finally rang. As the sky lightened Donna lay unsleeping, trying to fathom the meaning of the nightmare, trying to blur the details so the pictures and emotions would dim into dreamlike fantasy. It was impossible.

Wearily she got up and went to work.

When she saw Stephen the next evening, she could almost taste the fear. As he took her in his arms and his eyes probed hers, she saw his gaze darken and in one terrifying moment she knew the dream had been a remembrance of another reality.

She tried to struggle from his arms, tried to free herself and run, but his grip was binding. Too late, memories of a past life had returned to haunt her, too late to save her.

"Where's Henry?" Her voice sounded strange to her ears and his laugh shuddered through her mind.

"So, you've remembered."

She gazed into his beautiful eyes, and saw his cruel lust for revenge.

"I said I'd come back." His voice was soft in her ear, menacing, and his smile sent a chill through her heart.

Making Your Own Luck

I knew Hattie hadn't killed herself. It was the whisky; Hattie never drank whisky.

"Rob, it's Hattie." Mary's voice had been tearful on the phone. "I went in to clean as usual, like I always do on Tuesdays, and there she was, in her bed – I thought she was still asleep, so I spoke to her. 'Hattie,' I said. 'Hattie!' But she never answered and when I touched her she was so cold." Mary was sobbing now and I felt an icy hand clutch my stomach.

"I called the doctor and he rang all sorts of people, and now they're saying she might have killed herself. I don't know what to do, so I rang you, seeing as how you were here yesterday."

I shook my head to clear the panic. "Don't worry, Mary, I'm coming over."

I put the phone down and grabbed my coat.

I had been in Hattie's garden yesterday. Although it was April, there was a keen wind. It cut right through me when I tried to dig the soil for planting.

"I want the front bed full of dahlias, Rob." Hattie was sitting at the kitchen table with me, a notepad in front of her. Planning her garden was something she really enjoyed. Hattie wouldn't commit suicide in spring, not until the garden was planted to her liking. Besides, yesterday we'd ordered the dahlias.

I noticed her hands were shaking though. "Cold got to you,

Hattie?" I asked. Her arthritis had worsened over winter.

She nodded and sighed. "Sometimes I think peace is a long time coming." Her voice was sad. "I'll be ninety-four next month, Rob. That's a good few years on my own; and I've had enough. I'm ready when the good Lord is, I'm just waiting on Him." She smiled and her tired eyes sparkled. "In the meantime, let's be planning the garden."

I usually tended Hattie's garden once or twice a week, more in the summer. I knew she looked forward to my visits, and Mary's. Having no family she was interested in our lives.

She'd been that happy when I got engaged last autumn. I took Sadie round to see her and the next day Hattie was as excited as a kid at Christmas.

"I'm so glad for you, Rob. She's as pretty as a picture!" She winked at me and I swelled with pride.

'You make your own luck,' my father had always told me. I hadn't believed that until now. All the lads of the village fancied Sadie and she'd chosen me. I wasn't sure why. She met all sorts of interesting fellas through her job but now it was me she loved. I knew I was lucky, and I worked hard on being what she wanted. I might not have the looks, but I'd do anything for Sadie!

"You're dependable, Rob," she said. "I know I can trust you. And I want a husband I can trust. You'd make a good father too?" Her lips were close to mine and at that moment I'd have given her a dozen children if that was what she wanted.

"What about all them flash men you meet at work?"

"They're just passing through." She laughed. "They flirt and sometimes say they'll be back, but they're not *reliable*."

I nodded. Being a waitress at the Saucy Diner, she attracted attention in her red check pinny, that's for sure. But it was *me* she was promised to.

I just had one problem, which I confided to Hattie that day. "It's a ring, Hattie." I leaned forward. "I'm a bit pushed for money, being winter and work being scarce. How do I get her a ring?"

"Never you mind about that!" Hattie answered briskly and painfully levered herself from her chair with her stick. "I've just the thing."

She rummaged in her desk and produced a small box. Inside was the most beautiful diamond I had ever seen. I stared at Hattie in horror. "I can't take that off you," I spluttered. "I wasn't meaning..." I felt embarrassed. I had been looking for advice, not a handout.

"Don't you be silly, Rob." She pushed the box across the table. "You take that for your Sadie. It would make me happier than anything to know it was being worn again." She spread her fingers and the swollen knuckles cracked. "I shall never wear it again," she said ruefully. "And it would look a treat on your Sadie's finger."

I couldn't deny that. But to take Hattie's ring seemed wrong somehow. She sensed my discomfort and closed the box, taking my hand and resting it over it.

"It's yours, Rob," she said firmly. "I'll hear no more about it. You've given me a lot of fun with your company, and you've always done my garden a treat, just how I like it. Just one thing..." She paused, a smile in her eyes.

"What?"

"Bring Sadie with you when she's wearing the ring."

"Of course." I dropped a kiss on the wrinkled cheek and, putting the ring safely in my inside pocket, I went to get ready for the dahlias. Heart of gold, had Hattie. I mused on my good luck as I dug.

Just how much luck was coming my way I found out after I'd taken an ecstatic Sadie to see Hattie. I hadn't mentioned where I got the ring, it didn't seem appropriate somehow, and Hattie didn't let on, but she admired the ring on Sadie's slim finger and I saw a tear come in her eye. The next time I called she beckoned me in before I could put spade to soil.

"Rob, come in." She shut the door behind us and led the way into the kitchen. "I've got a surprise for you." She was excited and put a cup of tea in front of me before I could wipe my boots.

"Sit down," she commanded. I obeyed, wondering what was going on now.

"When are you getting wed?" She leaned forward, her eyes gleaming.

I shrugged. "Not too soon. We're going to save a bit and then, of course, we need a house…" She stopped me with a wave of her hand.

"Precisely." She grinned. She sat back and sipped her tea.

"So?" I was confused.

"I've not much longer left." She waved me quiet as I started to protest. "I want you and Sadie to have my house. Bring some life into these walls, children and laughter."

I was dumbfounded. Sadie and me had got our eyes on one of the little terraced houses on the edge of the town. About all we could afford really. But Hattie's house, with it's three bedrooms and large garden… I stared at Hattie, dumbstruck.

She laughed. "I was wondering what to do with it," she chuckled. "I've no family. Can't leave it to a dog's home, can I? You and Sadie would be just perfect."

"We can't!" I managed to squeak.

"Why not?"

I had no answer.

"It's all settled. We'll talk of it no more. Now…" She rose and opened the kitchen door. "Go and see to the garden."

I worked in a daze that morning. Talk about heart of gold! I thought about what Hattie had said all day, and all night, sleep being a long way off. By morning I'd come to a decision. I wouldn't tell Sadie about the house. What if I did and then found that Hattie was only having me on? No, best to wait and see what happened. There was no rush to get married; best to wait and see.

Then Sadie got pregnant. I was cross at first. After all, she said she'd taken care of that, and besides, we hadn't saved very much and how on earth could we afford to get married and look after a baby? I must admit I was scared. Sadie was all tearful and said she'd look awful in her pinny with a bulge and then she cried on my shoulder and said she knew she could rely on me to sort it all out; and I said 'Of course I would', all strong like, though inside I was all churned up. It's funny how your luck suddenly turns.

*

And now Mary said Hattie was dead. When I got to the house the police were there. That threw me a bit. This policeman took me into the kitchen and I looked round, expecting Hattie to be brewing tea by the window.

"Rob Jones, isn't it?" His voice was kind but his open notebook made me nervous. "You were here yesterday?"

I nodded and then, as he waited, "I dug the garden ready for the dahlias."

"And how did Hattie seem?"

I shrugged. "Bright as usual."

"She didn't seem depressed?" I shook my head.

"Hmm. Does she normally drink whisky?"

"She does have a wee drop now and then, when her arthritis is painful."

"You've seen her drink it? Only I understood she was teetotal?"

I shrugged. "She was in a lot of pain."

The officer made a note.

"Perhaps she took some to get to sleep?" I ventured, as he didn't speak.

"That seems possible." He sighed and snapped his book shut. "It seems to me she probably took a drop to sleep, and mixed with her tablets... She was very frail." He stood up. "Thanks for your help. We shan't be bothering you again. The doctor just wanted to be sure."

"Of course." I heaved a sigh of relief and stood up. "Dear Hattie, I shall miss her. Heart of gold, she had."

They all left and I crept upstairs to say goodbye before the undertaker arrived. She looked so peaceful lying there. I would put the whisky bottle back in the cupboard, where it had sat for years in case a guest arrived.

It had been at my instigation she had sipped a drop, to help her sleep, and it worked.

"I need a nap, Rob," she called from the kitchen door. "I'm feeling all about, I need to lie down."

"I'll bring you some hot milk," I promised.

Leaving my spade, I heated milk in the saucepan. My mind had been going all morning, out in the cold sunshine, going over and over my problem, and now I suddenly saw a solution. I mixed some of the whisky with the drink and took it upstairs.

"This'll help you rest, Hattie." She sniffed and a frown crinkled her brow.

"Drink, Hattie." I held her thin shoulders and almost poured the drink down her throat. Gently I laid her back on the pillow.

"You're a good boy, Rob." Her speech was slurred and she slipped into sleep like a baby.

Now, I straightened the pillow, smoothing the wrinkles. That was when I had panicked yesterday, putting the pillow back behind her head, and I forgot to return the whisky.

It had been so simple and the pillow was soft; it wouldn't have hurt her. I couldn't see her face as she slipped away. I liked to think that I'd helped her find the peace that she'd been waiting so patiently for; that made it easier to come to terms with her death.

"Thank you, Hattie." I kissed the cold cheek and went back downstairs.

Letting myself out of the house I popped the spare key in my pocket. I would need that. I squared my shoulders and walked away.

'You make your own luck,' my father's voice echoed in my head. He was right.

I must ring Sadie and tell her we'd be getting wed as soon as we could fix the date.

A Raw Talent

Three of the travellers passed me by as I wrestled with the key in my shop door. The father never spared me a glance; thin, leaning to the shape of his greyhound slinking light-foot at his side. A cigarette drooped, sodden as the man's hair, and his eyes were dull, watching the distance as his hand limply clasped the lead.

By his side a sturdy youngster; baby-fat legs toddling to keep pace, cherub hands clinging to the chain of a smaller animal, some semblance of a dog in the furry coat and lolling tongue, his pedigree distilled over many matings. The child's eyes still held innocence and wonder as he gazed at the sun-washed gardens, the spring flowers sparkling with dew, nodding in the gentle breeze. A smile played around his mouth as his breath panted. The dog pulled him forward.

Behind, a gangly youth tarried. He watched as I fitted the key. I smiled at him to dispel my nervousness. His ragged clothes, too small for his bony frame, wafted the smell of the hedgerows to my nostrils and his skin clung to fine bones. His eyes were wistful and sheered away from my smile, slid to the shop window and gazed hungrily at the paintings displayed. Grimy fingers reached for the glass as if trying to touch the colours and his shoulders heaved in a sigh.

"How much for the watercolour?" His voice was hesitant, surprisingly mellow and I paused as the door swung open. The paintings were originals, expensive, but his longing was obvious.

And he had called them watercolours, correctly.

"The prices are all different. Come inside and have a look."

I knew I was being foolish, following my instincts again instead of thinking sensibly. But it was too late. He stepped through the doorway behind me and, out of the corner of my eye, I saw the two dog-walkers disappear over the brow of the hill. We were alone, the boy and I, alone among the treasures of art, and I took a deep breath to still the uneasiness that hovered on the edge of my mind.

He didn't touch the displayed paintings, but his eyes caressed the brush strokes, his tongue following the lines of his thin mouth as his body hunched towards the watercolours.

"Too expensive." He sighed quietly, a look of resignation wafting fleetingly over his features. He hadn't expected otherwise.

"Do you paint?" I was curious and watched him as I opened the shutters, sunlight splaying over the canvases. I switched on display lights and noticed he recoiled from the glare.

He shrugged. "I did, once. Haven't any paints now."

"The local college holds courses. Would you like to enrol for one?" I held out a leaflet, an artist beaming colourfully on the cover.

His wistful look turned to derision. "I couldn't afford to!" He almost spat the words and I flinched. I hadn't meant to humiliate him.

"I'm sorry," I mumbled and turned away, concentrating on opening drawers, taking out pad and pencil, showing business professionalism; wishing he would leave.

"I could do odd jobs for you? I work hard."

I stared at him, confused. He wanted work? I shook my head and his shoulders slumped. "Thought not."

The doorbell clanged and the old wooden doorframe rattled as he released his anger. He didn't glance again in the window as he scurried up the road.

The encounter had shaken me; me, the independent career woman, proving myself as good as any man in business; me and my powerful equilibrium, disturbed by a ragamuffin.

For the first time in thirteen years my fingers itched to paint, to expel the emotions that overwhelmed me, onto paper. I clenched my fists in denial. I never wanted to hold a brush again. Grief had dispelled my talent and I had no wish to suffer further frustration through any attempts to paint again. My creative days were over. Now I took my joy in other artists' work.

I watched for him next day. This time he was alone, leading a lurcher. "You could mow the lawns if you like. Dig the flower beds."

I stood on the pavement blocking his passage. His expression was surly and I felt colour flame my cheeks. I thought he was going to step around me but suddenly, a thin smile lit his face and his eyes seemed to waken.

"You'll pay me?"

I nodded, aware of the disapproving look shot with venom by my neighbour. "I'll pay. What's your name?"

He hesitated. "Reuben. I'll be back later."

He continued on his way and a wave of anger rushed through my mind. "Fool," I muttered as I re-entered the shop. "You're a fool."

He was surprisingly agile in the garden. Soil turned, weeds stacked in neat tumps and flowers spread their leaves in relief. I watched his thin body coil over his labour. When he rested on the grass I took him tea and biscuits and sat besides him, unsure of myself.

"I should like to see you paint."

He dunked a biscuit and caught the soggy mass with his tongue. "Have you any paints I could use?"

I fetched paper and half-used tubes of pigments. I set up a small easel and gestured to him. "Take an hour out, paint me a picture." I walked away before he could refuse.

His face was stiff with concentration. His eyes flicked from garden to paper and his fine fingers moved with gentle precision.

It was several hours later when I allowed myself to creep behind his shoulders. I was amazed.

He had captured the euphorial hues of the buds, his grass was alive with the wind, and the imaginary tree shading the meadow my lawn had become was majestic in its spring splendour. A figure strode across the field, upright, free, hair tossed by the breeze, and running ahead was a dog, a beautiful golden Labrador, its tail swaying joyfully, its tongue lolling in happiness. I was spellbound.

"Where did you learn to paint like that?" His gifted talent excited me.

He shrugged. "I lived with my grandmother for a while, in a house. She painted and I copied."

"You don't live with her now?"

"She's dead. Don't have time to paint, or money to buy paper."

"Sign it," I instructed. "In the right-hand corner."

He looked uncomfortable.

"Just your first name, Reuben."

He held the brush aloft for a moment and then marked a sloping *R* and a squiggle.

"Very artistic." I smiled. "You must come again."

He jumped to his feet. "You said you'd pay me. I must get back."

He followed me to the house and stood at the door.

"Come in." I walked through to the kitchen.

Warily, he followed, his eyes afraid as he stared at the windows and he shivered as the door slammed behind him in the breeze. The key fell from its hiding place on the ledge of the doorframe and he picked it up, slowly placing it on the table. His eyes never left the door. Then he reached for the handle and opened it, watching it, hands dug deep in his pockets, until he was sure it would stay for him to escape. I smelt his fear. Breathing quickly he snatched the coins and turned, his steps reaching for the freedom beyond the walls.

"Will you come again? What about your painting?"

I saw him shake his head as he ran across the grass towards the gate, and his foot kicked the pigments beside his easel and scattered them. A great sadness welled in my heart and I gathered his borrowed materials and took the painting through to the gallery.

I found a wooden frame to fit his picture and hung it on the wall. It was quite beautiful. He would only be about thirteen, maybe older. Thirteen. Thirteen years; had it really been that long?

I had loved this shop the moment I set eyes on it. I was on holiday, touring aimlessly through the lush countryside, seeking solace for my hurt. I took a room in the village; the shop was for sale. It was a spur of the moment decision, a crazy madness that saw me moving within days to the other end of the country, my past a shadow in my mind.

It took thirteen years to build up my stock of watercolours. Collectors began to know my name, I was commissioned for special purchases, but I never picked up a brush again myself.

Now Reuben had rekindled that old yearning and my fingers traced his brushstrokes. Could I still paint? Was I strong enough to try? Thirteen years was a long time. Had my life been different it would have been my son holding the brush and mixing colours; I liked to think he would have inherited my talent, had he come alive into this world. Maybe he wouldn't have had the gift, but I would still have loved him.

I suppose I knew in my heart that Reuben wouldn't come back. As I walked to work the next day the neighbour told me the travellers had moved out.

"Good job too," she said. "Made a right mess of the meadow, they did. Left piles of rubbish and several hens are missing!"

I smiled politely and strode across the garden. The kitchen door swung open at my touch and a shaft of fear speared my mind. Slowly I walked through to the gallery. The paintings had gone, all but one. His painting hung crookedly, alone on the magnolia wall, surrounded by dust squares where the watercolours had been. I took the painting down and carried it to the kitchen where I hid it in a cupboard; then I phoned the police.

The insurance company wasn't happy. There had been no break-in; the kitchen door had been unlocked. The stern police officer pointed out the folly of hiding a key on top of a rickety doorframe.

"One shake," he pushed against the door to emphasise his point, "one shake and the key would fall. And look at that gap!" He pointed to the space below the door. "Slip the key from under and there you are, easy pickings."

I didn't say a word. He was right. I should have been more careful, hidden the key better, especially after... I saw Reuben standing in my kitchen, heard the wind bang the door and the rattle of the key as it fell. Of course, it might not have been the travellers. There had been several thefts in recent weeks, and they had all been attributed to the wide boys in the nearby town.

"Had any dubious callers lately?"

I shook my head and he sighed. "Ah well." He snapped his book shut and stood up. "I should replace that door, get some security locks."

I nodded and showed him out. I knew I would never see my paintings again.

I recouped some of my losses. I cleaned the walls and built shelves to carry bric-a-brac for the tourists. I bought cheap paintings from local artists and recovered the walls. His picture I hung high, almost to the rafters, where the late sunbeams caught the golden hair of the dog, and brought alive a meadow in the beamed shadows. Several tourists liked the painting.

"It's not for sale," I said, studying the *R* and squiggle that spoke of Reuben. "It's not for sale." And they would turn away, disappointed.

I suppose you could say it's an original, a unique original. Maybe one day it will be valuable. Maybe one day Reuben will come back and the deep ache in my heart will ease.

But somehow, as I sit at my easel in the garden, my hesitant hand splashing watercolours across the canvas, I doubt it.

Over the Rainbow

Sarah stood in the archway and gazed at the rainbow looping the Manor with its brilliance, mirrored colours shimmering on the old stones. It dipped behind the hedge, the pot of gold hidden.

"In the pool," Sarah murmured to herself. "Andrew said the pot of gold would land in the pool one day, and we would dive for the treasure!"

She smiled as she remembered their childhood whisperings as they had sat on the rickety bench by the pool. It had been their secret place and had heard her innermost dreams, her ambitions as she had matured.

"See," Andrew spoke softly, that last day together before she had gone to college, "there's a rainbow, Sarah, to bring you luck."

There had indeed been a rainbow, the brightest they had ever seen. The Manor behind them had been black in the shadows of the retreating storm, but over the pool the sun shone and a rainbow lit the hills in the distance.

"It's so far away," Sarah sighed.

"It'll come to the pool one day, you'll see." Andrew had always been the optimist, cheering her when she was down, bolstering her confidence.

That first day, when she and her parents arrived at the stone cottage in the grounds and moved all her treasured possessions into her strange new bedroom, she had been scared. The Manor looked enormous and very frightening to a six year old. She had been sent to explore.

"Not far away mind," her mother admonished. "Take a look around while we get sorted. I need to get organised before your Dad starts work tomorrow."

Sarah crept through the imposing gardens and spied the gate in the dense hedge. She ignored the *Private* sign and slipped through. Before her spread the lake, sunlight glistening on the water and yellow celandines spraying gold around the edge. On the banks there were flowers of all colours, pink and blue and white and, to Sarah, it seemed a magical place.

A mother duck paddled serenely across the water, behind her a gaggle of fluffy ducklings, splattering their way in a frantic effort to keep up with their mother's measured paddles. Sarah laughed delightedly.

Perhaps her new home wasn't so bad after all. This would be her secret place, her hideaway. She walked slowly forward and spotted a bench, leaning lopsidedly over some cowslips. Gingerly, she sat down. Although it creaked, it didn't move, and she relaxed.

She didn't notice the boy, so engrossed was she in the beauty before her, until the bench creaked again and she felt the warmth of his body beside her.

"Who are you?" She was startled and gazed at him fearfully.

"I'm Andrew." He smiled gently at her and her fear melted. "I saw you arrive."

"You did?"

He nodded and waved his hand towards the Manor. "That's my family home."

"Oh!"

"It's all right." Andrew smiled again. "I don't mind you being here, I love this place too."

"You do?"

He nodded emphatically. "I often come here when I feel lonely."

Sarah gazed at him. He was taller than her, with dark curls running carelessly over his forehead and his eyes were the bluest she had ever seen.

"Can I come here too?" She ventured at last.

"Of course. Whenever you want. I'll always come as well, if you like."

Sarah nodded. "Yes please." She jumped up hurriedly. "I'd better go. Mum will wonder where I am. See you soon, Andrew." She felt suddenly shy and skipped away, leaving Andrew staring at the lake.

A storm was hovering on the hills and, as she turned to wave, she glimpsed a rainbow in the smooth water.

On her sixteenth birthday she had said a sad farewell.

"You'll love college." Andrew was enthusiastic. "Think of all the new friends you'll make, think of the parties."

"I'll miss you though."

He took her hand and splayed her fingers across his palm. "I'll miss you." His voice was soft. "But it's time for you to move on, explore the world. There's a whole new life out there, just waiting for you. Grab it with both hands, Sarah, enjoy every precious moment." His voice had an urgency that startled her.

"Wear this," he slipped a ring from his finger, "and I'll always be with you."

Sarah surveyed the ring on her index finger.

"It's beautiful," she whispered. "Are you sure?"

He nodded and caressed her finger for a moment. "I'm sure, and it'll bring you back to me one day."

All that had been a long time ago and Sarah stood now, twisting the same ring on her little finger. She wore it always as she had promised, a symbol of remembrance and it had been much admired; an aquamarine set in intricate gold weavings of snakes and crowns. She stared at the rainbow, fading slightly, that dipped towards her pool. She wondered if Andrew was sitting on the bench watching it and then shook herself.

"Don't be silly!" She grinned to herself.

It had been so long since she had been home and the Manor had changed hands. A distant relation had bought it and, for a while, the gardens had been closed. Her parents had retired and returned north and there had been no reason to return.

And then, one day, visiting a friend nearby, she had read that the gardens were once again open to the public and she had felt a sudden yearning to see her home again. Taking a room at the local inn, she decided to stay a few days and, that first night, she had dreamed of Andrew.

Slowly she walked up the gravel drive. The gardens looked immaculate as usual and a few early visitors straggled the paths. She came to the gate, almost hidden now by the hedge, the *Private* sign newly painted, and pushed it open.

The path was overgrown but the lake was still there, smaller than she remembered, yellow iris now claiming a large proportion of the water. There was no sign of the ducks.

The seat had been mended with odd bits of wood, but still creaked as she sat down. She felt sadness creep over her as she noticed the rainbow had disappeared, swallowed by the sun, and the pot of gold was as illusive as ever.

"Where are you, Andrew?" she whispered, almost expecting to feel his body fill the seat next to her.

She was so lost in memories that she didn't hear the soft footsteps on the grass or see the tall figure at her side until he spoke.

"Excuse me." His voice was gentle and she swung round, startled.

Staring into the sun, she thought it was Andrew, a grown-up Andrew, with his dark curls slightly shorter, but his eyes, his eyes were the same brilliant blue that she remembered.

"Andrew?" She shot to her feet, her heart thumping and the man at her side smiled down at her.

"I'm afraid not!"

She saw at once that she was mistaken and coloured. "I'm sorry…" she floundered, completely confused.

"Mark." He held out his hand.

"Sarah."

For a moment their hands stayed intertwined and she was aware of the warmth.

"I saw you come through the gate." He was watching her. "It does say *Private*."

She nodded.

"It says private for a reason," he explained as if she were a child and she felt her senses return to normal. "This part of the grounds really isn't safe for visitors. The lake," he gestured towards the water, "it isn't fenced and there was an accident here once."

"I know." She smiled her most winsome smile, once more in command of the situation. "I do apologise, but my parents worked here a few years ago. As a child I grew up here, and this was my secret place."

"Ah!" His face cleared. "So you're Sarah."

She was startled. "How do you know?"

He grinned. "Come," he said without further explanation, "let's go and have a coffee, and you can tell me what you've been doing since you left."

Mystified, she followed Mark back through the hedge to the chatter of the tourists. The sun was bathing the old walls in golden light and the rainbow glowed faintly over the far hills.

He led the way to the café, tucked away in the remains of the old walled garden. Clematis festooned the stones and hollyhocks and roses scented the air. Leaving him to order the coffee, she selected a table near the window and gazed across the sunny lawns.

She watched him as he waited in the queue. He was certainly an attractive man, much as she imagined Andrew would have been. She wondered if Mark was married and blushed at her thoughts. As if sensing her attention he turned towards her and, just for a moment, their eyes met and she felt a lurch in her heart.

"Coffee, and I've treated us to two of the homemade cakes."

She looked at the sponges, oozing cream and jam and chuckled. "I shan't say no. Thanks."

He sat down. "So," he leaned across the table, fixing her with the brilliance of his eyes, "what have you done since you left here?"

"I've completed my course at College, travelled some, and now, well…"

"Now?"

"I'm not sure." Her eyes met his. "How did you know who I was?"

"I saw your photo."

"My photo!" Sarah was startled. "Where?"

"In a drawer in a bedroom. It must have been put away and forgotten."

"Who by?"

Mark shrugged and grinned. "I don't know. But whoever it was did me a favour. Come on, eat up, and then I'll show you."

They walked across the lawns to the Manor and Sarah felt her heart thump as he pushed open the old oak door. The hallway was as she remembered it, glass chandeliers and mellow wood, a spiral staircase wending its way to the next floor. She'd always thought the Manor elegant, timeless and, as she followed Mark up the wooden stairs, she felt as if she had come home.

They entered one of the rooms at the front of the house, its bay window opening towards the pool, and she had a glimpse of water mirrored in the glass. Mark opened a drawer and took out a photo. Sarah gazed at her younger self; she must have been about fifteen, sitting on the bench gazing into the pool, her face a study in sereneness. She was alone and wondered who had taken the photo. She had no recollection of the event and a shiver ran up her spine.

"That's me all right!" She laughed, but couldn't keep the slight shake from her voice. "I wonder when that was taken? I certainly don't remember it." She turned the photo over and there, in a sloping scrawl, was written '*Sarah, waiting for her rainbow*'.

She handed it back to Mark. At least that explained how he knew who she was.

She turned and left the room, suddenly anxious to return to the sunshine. Mark followed and they stopped on the landing, studying the portraits of the family through the ages. Halfway along there was a painting of Andrew as a child.

"Andrew Coker." Mark spoke softly behind her.

"You look like him." Sarah was studying the familiar face.

"So I'm told. Poor Andrew. You know he was only sixteen when he died."

"The accident in the lake," Sarah's voice was husky. "He was looking for his pot of gold."

Sarah felt the tears prick her eyes as her finger caressed the familiar face and traced his cheek, dropping gently to the ring adorning the folded hand. She read the brass plaque in a whisper.

'*Andrew Coker 1740 – 1756*'

A shadow moved on the landing and a photograph fluttered to the floor.

Rushed to Death

"It's a foggy morning," Susan commented brightly, as she peered through the window at the early morning gloom. "You'd better get a move on, John."

Her husband groaned and heaved himself from the warm bed. It didn't seem that long since he'd fallen into an exhausted sleep. He tottered to the bathroom.

"Got to rush." His kiss glanced off her cheek as he hurried through the door.

Susan watched him run down the path. The car revved and was quickly lost in the swirling fog. Sighing, she closed the front door. The years were rushing by so quickly; and they still hadn't started the family she longed for!

"One day, when things ease up," John promised each time she broached the subject, but that time never seemed to come. She appreciated he was working hard to make his advertising agency a success, but she felt she was losing her husband and dreams in the process.

John peered through the dense fog as he slowly joined the queue of crawling traffic leaving the suburbs, following the hazy tail light in front of him. He drummed his fingers on the steering wheel and fiddled with the radio. The local station warned of hazardous fog and long tailbacks. He switched off impatiently.

He had an appointment that morning with Mr Rogers,

hopefully a new client, and cursed the fact that he'd left his mobile on charge in the office.

He felt the familiar irritation chase through his mind, the tension tightening his muscles. A new client was important. If he got this contract he might be able to ease up a bit, spend some time with Susan. She had been very quiet lately and he was worried.

At that moment the car in front shot forward. He thrust his foot on the accelerator. Lights flashed. Horns sounded.

Shadowy houses caught his eye – the fog was lifting. John breathed a sigh of relief. The car he was following made a sharp turn and disappeared.

Suddenly the road in front was clear; no fog, no traffic. John braked sharply as a large sign blocked his way. *ROAD CLOSED.*

"Damn!" Somehow he must have missed the diversion. "Damn, damn!"

He looked around. He was in an unfamiliar road. Small cottages on either side, a village ahead. He could see the spire of the church glinting in the sunlight. The grass sparkled with dampness and the air felt fresh and clean.

He sat for a moment. Obviously he had taken a turning off the main road. He couldn't remember doing so, but the fog must have disorientated him, made him lose his sense of direction. Heaven only knew where he was!

Stemming the tide of angry panic he tried to think rationally. He was lost. The most sensible thing to do was to find out where he was and plan his route accordingly. He got out of the car and locked the door, setting off at a brisk pace. His stomach felt knotted and his head had started to ache.

The sun was warm on his shoulders and he felt the peaceful atmosphere of the village enfold him as he walked along the cobbled street. A young lad was whistling cheerfully as he ambled along.

"Excuse me…" The lad smiled and stopped. John noticed his arm was in a sling. "Can you tell me where I am? I appear to be lost!"

The boy's voice was gentle, as he looked John up and down.

"You are indeed lost, unusually so!"

"I need to get back to the main road. Is it far from here?"

The lad shook his head. "I'm sorry, I really don't know. I haven't been here very long, can't go far with this arm." He raised the plastered limb. "I broke it, rushing to school. I was always late. Now look at me!" He grinned and sauntered off.

John quickened his pace irritably. Surely there was someone about who could give him directions?

He noticed a postman, a mailbag swinging from his shoulder. He was limping and leaning on a stick.

"Should you be carrying that heavy bag?" John's concern overrode his irritation as he touched the elderly man on the arm.

The man smiled placidly at him. "It isn't so heavy, and it's my own fault! I was rushing, I had so much post to deliver." He sighed. "Wasn't concentrating on the road, only on my deliveries; the van driver didn't stand a chance. My own fault. Can't rush now though!"

He chuckled as he hobbled off, leaving John standing there, bemused. He'd forgotten to ask for directions! Lethargy was creeping over him as he wandered on.

What a lovely place to live. He must bring Susan, have a look at houses for sale, it would be such a healthy place to bring up a family.

He caught sight of a young lady pushing a pram. "Excuse me, my dear."

She stopped and greeted him as everyone else had, with a welcoming smile, no fear for the stranger showing in her glowing eyes.

"How can I help you?" Her voice had a musical lilt and he couldn't resist a glance at the baby in the pram, unfamiliar feelings stirring as he looked at the sleeping face, heavily shrouded in woollen blankets. The mother pulled the covering down a little so that he could see the child.

"My son," she said with pride. "He's been unwell, so I don't want him to catch a cold. We've both been unwell. I went rushing out shopping without a coat, caught a chill, too busy to take care of myself; and then he caught it too. A vicious bug it was, but we're fine now. He's so precious." She smiled sweetly at John.

"Beautiful," he agreed, staring at the babe. "Now," he spoke firmly with an effort, "I appear to be lost. I took a wrong turning in the fog and found myself here. Unfortunately, pleasant though it is, I need to get to work. Can you possibly direct me back to the main road?"

"You have a car? Have you had an accident?"

"Not quite!" John laughed as he remembered the flashing lights and squealing brakes. "No, my car's on the edge of the village. The sign said *ROAD CLOSED*, so I left it there and here I am! But I need to return." He was aware that he was gabbling.

"Most unusual!" Her quiet voice was interested and her eyes swept over him. "A visitor. How strange!"

John was beginning to feel very strange himself and extremely bewildered.

"Can you tell me how to get back?" His voice was filled with anxiety and she sighed.

"Of course," she said. "If you must."

"Oh, I must!" he said, with more confidence than he felt.

"Then," she smiled, "go back to your car and turn around. Follow the lane and you'll find the main road. But please don't rush. There's so little time if you rush."

She walked on, crooning to the baby and John turned and strode resolutely to his car. He did a three-point turn at remarkable speed and headed back along the lane. Glancing in the mirror, he was annoyed to see the fog had descended again and the village was totally obscured.

"Don't rush!" Her soft voice whispered in his head, but he felt his irritation erasing her gentle words. He glanced at his watch and was even more annoyed to find it had stopped at a quarter to nine.

In a short space of time, he saw the main road and queues of slow moving traffic. Sighing resignedly, he edged into the flow.

"Good morning, Mr Mansell." Janice, his secretary, greeted him cheerfully. "Glad to see you made it, despite the fog!"

"Mr Rogers?"

"Mr Rogers phoned to say he'd be a few minutes late. Delayed by the weather. I said you'd understand."

"A few minutes…" He glanced at his watch again. "What time is it?"

"Ten past nine."

"Ten past nine?" he repeated, astonished.

She nodded and followed him in to his office. "I'll just go through the post and get you a coffee. There should be time before Mr Rogers arrives."

John hardly heard her. He was staring at his watch. It said ten past nine.

He sat down slowly, gazing through his window at the foggy mass that swirled and clung to the buildings, but in his mind he saw the village bathed in sunshine – had it been real? Time belied his visit, but…

'Don't rush.' Her words echoed clearly in his head. 'There is so little time if you rush.'

A strange feeling of elation swept through him. He had been lost, not just this morning but for a long time; lost in a fog of rush and hurry, his life hurtling by. But he was lucky, he had another chance…

He saw a shaft of sunshine brush his window and smiled. At last the fog was lifting. He picked up the internal phone.

"Janice, cancel my afternoon appointments. I'm going home early. Get me Susan on the phone please."

Tunnel of Dreams

"**J**enny, Jenny!" The echoes were derisive. I peered into the darkness of the tunnel, almost expecting to hear the thunder of a train, but the rails had long since been torn from the shaled ground. Now nettles stung my sandalled feet.

A man in sandals! Jenny had been scornful.

"Jenny, please come back." My voice hollowed and floated, repeating; gone. As Jenny was gone.

Why did she have to be so brave, and make me feel so cowardly? I just couldn't go through the tunnel. But Jenny could, and had, her laughter echoing as her shadow merged into the mantling greyness, laughter that mocked and died to a whisper as she ran further, until only a breath of feathered wind touched my cheek.

And then she rounded the bend and obscurity settled gently before my eyes. I hesitated, on the brink of floundering into nothingness, but fear held me back. Even as a child I had been afraid to explore the depths of the tunnel.

All the lads of our gang goaded one another, taunted, but not one of us ever ventured into the gloom of that tunnel. It was the curve; it hid that encouraging dot of distant light that proclaimed the tunnel ended. And so we peered, schemed and bragged; but never quite dared.

I remember searching for the other end. It had to be

somewhere in those rocky hills. But I never found it and soon tired of so boring a game. There was too much else to do. My childhood was bleak enough without dwelling on cavernous, endless tunnels.

But the tunnel that was in the picture that hung at the foot of my bed was different. That domed entrance covered rails and a bright green engine chugging happily into it, sculptured smoke puffing into blue sky, immobilised in water colours by some unknown hand, fated never to reach the end of its tunnel either. There was only one carriage on the train, but that startling red carriage with unlikely sparkling windows carried my dreams.

It was Uncle Ted who gave me the picture. Uncle Ted, my mother's brother, yet so different from my mother. When he came to stay, life was fun. He would tease and run, hide until I cried with frustration and then he'd gallop crazily through the house with me clinging precariously to his back uttering shrieks of excited fright. The days would end in hysterical happiness and mother would admonish us both.

"Over-exciting the boy, Edward! Not good for him." And she'd snort disapprovingly and Uncle Ted would look shamefaced and wink slyly at me, and I'd feel the importance of being his ally in misdemeanour.

It was Uncle Ted who heard me cry out in the night, the horror of nightmare leaving me damp and shaking.

"Another weakness!" A sniff showed mother's disapproval when Uncle Ted mentioned my fear next morning.

The following night he woke me when he crept into my room.

"Here, Patrick," he whispered conspiratorially, and undid crackling brown paper. It was the picture.

He removed the smirking cat from the foot of my bed and hung the glowing train. The faint light from the window cast shadows and made it seem real.

"Now, Patrick," he looked at me solemnly, "when you feel afraid, you just concentrate on the train, because this train is magic!"

I gazed at it in awe, but saw nothing strange. "How, Uncle?"

"If you pretend, very hard, to step into that carriage, and then close your eyes, the train will glide through the tunnel and take you wherever you wish to go."

"It will?"

Uncle Ted nodded. "But you must concentrate completely on where you want to be, let your imagination take control."

I felt excited. "Can I try it tonight?"

"Shush!" He smiled a warning. "Your mother might hear. Don't forget..." He rose. "It's our secret!" And he sneaked stealthily away.

I think that was the first happy night of my young life. I lay and squeezed my eyes tightly shut and pretended. And, oh, the places I visited – imaginary castles of splendour; big houses full of warmth and food. I even thought I might visit my father, but I left that for another night.

Towards dawn my thoughts wandered. My father, he must have loved my mother once, mustn't he? I liked to think he had and I tried to remember the dusty image on the torn photograph my mother had shredded. The train did help.

I tried to imagine my mother as lovable. I knew I made her life difficult, but when I tried to help... Ah, well, perhaps one day I would understand why she disliked me so.

At least Uncle Ted liked me. He promised I should go and stay with him; sometime. I wasn't sure where he lived but I knew it must be a happy place. It sounded full of laughter and love. So many people living together with staff to care for them, albeit different ones as time went by.

But there was always Matron Jones. Uncle Ted loved Matron Jones. She had stayed with him through the years and he spoke fondly of her. I tried to speak fondly of mother, but she always moaned when Uncle Ted came to stay.

"Another child to mind!" she'd sigh. "Another worry."

But Uncle Ted was such fun! We understood each other, Uncle Ted and I. I would always remember the glorious hours of his visits. It was often on those memories that I slept.

★

I missed Uncle Ted when he moved away. Matron Jones had died and, for some reason, he moved house. It was too far away for him to visit very often. Mother seemed relieved.

It took me a while to realise I could visit him at night through the tunnel and, beneath the blankets, I'd relive the piggy-backs and jollity; only it wasn't quite the same and, come morning, I was beset by loneliness again.

It was a long time before I gave up hope of another, real, visit.

As I grew older my dreams changed and now I winged myself through exams, became someone important, maybe even famous. I joined the local theatrical society and dreamed of being spotted, my talent transporting me to stardom.

Alas for dreams. The day I started pulling levers on an oily machine in the local engineering factory I abandoned my train. Dreams held disillusionment.

And then came Jenny.

One night she knocked on the door. She had heard we had a spare room to let. A friend of my mother's had recommended us. My mother took her in.

I fell in love. Blue, innocent eyes and blond hair; she was all I ever wanted. For once my dreams came true. She loved me in return.

We'd wander through the hills together, so happy, sharing precious thoughts, and the old tunnel fascinated her.

"Let's go through, Patrick, please!"

I'd shake my head, unable to conquer my lingering childhood fear.

"One day, Jenny, one day," I promised.

Only she had tired of waiting, of promises, and now she had gone through the tunnel, alone. I felt wretched.

Suddenly I started running. Perhaps Jenny had come out of the other end of the tunnel and had raced me home! She'd be waiting, laughing delightedly at my frantic panic, proud of her achievement

– disdainful of my cowardice.

Of course she'd be waiting, of course she would!

My thumping heart repeated the promise as I rushed through the streets, gasping, mindless of traffic. I had to get home to Jenny.

I could hardly speak as I burst into the kitchen. Surprise flickered across my mother's lined face.

"Where's Jenny? Is she here?"

"Jenny!" Mother sighed in exasperation and banged a pan onto the cooker. "Now what stupid rubbish is filling your head, my lad? What ridiculous nonsense are you talking now?"

"Jenny?" I looked around, fear lurching in the base of my stomach and swelling into my throat.

"Jenny who?" Mother deftly peeled potatoes and they clattered dully into the saucepan.

"Jenny, who lives in our spare room."

"Have you finally taken leave of your senses, boy? We don't have a spare room. I wish to goodness we did! A lodger might help matters, make ends meet."

Her grumbling drifted through my head as I dragged myself up the stairs. We didn't have a spare room. I knew that, didn't I? Hadn't I always slept on the camp bed next to Uncle Ted when he came to stay? He used to curl up tightly beneath my sheets, my bunk too small for his heavy length: didn't he?

I studied the picture, and waited for the night. I wondered if Uncle Ted was still there, through the tunnel; and was Jenny with him?

Don't Go Back

He stopped on the dirt track, the dust billowing over his sandals, and listened. The laughter wafted through the olive blossom and swayed on the breeze, buoyed by the heady scent; a light joyous laughter that squeezed his heart and brought a lump to his throat.

He felt tears beneath his eyelids. How could he cry when the laughter conveyed so much joy? He pictured a young Greek girl, working in her garden, her homely Kalivi hidden from his eyes in the olive grove and he couldn't stop the memories crowding his senses, the image of Loukia filling his mind; the pain a physical blow.

"You must be daft, Greg!" His friend and colleague, Peter, had looked at him in surprise. "What on earth do you want to go back to Skopelos for?"

"It was a good holiday," Greg muttered.

"But, to go alone?" Peter took a swig of beer as he watched Greg over the rim. "You're not still hankering for the Greek girl – what was her name?"

"Loukia," Greg replied quietly and stared into his glass, running his finger over the handle. "Loukia."

"Let her go." Peter's voice was gentle. "It's not a good idea to go back."

Greg shrugged. Peter didn't know…

★

Greg ignored his friend's advice. He booked his flight, reserved an apartment and now, here he was, traipsing the ancient roads, searching for Loukia. He knew he was near her village – and then he heard the laughter.

Leaving the path he lurched down through the gnarled olive trees, the dust from the blossom making him sneeze as his shoulders brushed the branches. Thistles pierced his legs and flies swarmed angrily at the disturbance.

He stopped and listened. The laughter was fainter, fading. Panic-stricken he surged forward – and then it had gone. He waited as birdsong sped to the skies and the hum of bees in the scarlet poppies filled the air.

Resolutely, he ploughed on. There had to be a dwelling somewhere. But there was nothing but trees and poppy-filled grass clumps. Eventually he found himself, tired and disgruntled, his feet sore and bitten, on the lower road.

The next day he took a bus to her village. He sat outside the taverna and surveyed the scene. Boats rocked lazily on the swell of the sea, sun glistened on the white walls of the huddled houses, their terracotta roofs chequering up the pine-clad mountains that reared to the startling sky.

He watched the Greek lads, slouched at the next table. They were talking about him, heads close, voices low. They sat back, openly staring, and Greg shifted uncomfortably, concentrating his gaze on the ambling water.

Then one of them unwound himself from his chair and approached. For a moment fear tickled Greg's brain as the surly Greek drew near. Greg smiled apprehensively. Suddenly a grin turned the intimidating look to one of glee and Greg breathed a sigh of relief as he recognised him.

"Greg. Is Greg, yes?" The Greek held out his large hand and clasped Greg's. "Yassou, welcome back. You remember me, yes? Pavlos?

"Of course." Greg stood up. He recalled Loukia pointing him

out, her brother.

Pavlos gestured him to sit. "You stay?"

"One week."

Pavlos nodded.

"Loukia. Is she here?"

The grin disappeared and Pavlos slid into a seat. "Loukia is gone."

"Gone?"

Pavlos waved his arm about. "Gone, from the island." He shrugged, watching Greg, his eyes narrowed.

"She's coming back?" Greg could hear the panic in his voice.

"Who knows?" The grin spread again. "For you, maybe."

Pavlos stood and wandered back to his friends. He spoke harshly in his native tongue and they all rose and walked away. He heard their laughter as they kicked stones along the street, and he felt despondent.

As he sipped his Methos, he pondered. Perhaps Pavlos would tell Loukia he was here and she would return. His spirits lifted. If she had gone to the mainland it was only a short ferry ride home. All he could do was wait. He should have asked for her phone number, but the news had momentarily nonplussed him.

Why hadn't he left a contact address, a phone number, before he left? He and Peter hadn't intended to go to Skopelos – it was too quiet for their tastes – but, at short notice, it was all there was on offer. He needed the break. Training as a manager in the retail business had drained him; he was making mistakes, drinking too much…

When Peter suggested a few days in the sun, Greg jumped at the chance. The village near Skopelos town was small, their studio cramped, but on that first night they had gone to the taverna and the locals had made them welcome. Loukia was amongst them, with her brother, Pavlos, and his friends.

Shyly, with Greg's encouragement, she practised her broken English. They laughed a lot that night and Loukia promised to show him round, take him to a nightclub in Skopelos… He was entranced by her sweetness, his responses surprising him and, as the week flew by, he became afraid. He didn't want complications and Loukia was invading his soul.

That last night he had been so drunk. Her large eyes grew worried. He suggested a walk – to clear his head. She clung to his arm as they pushed through the soft grass beneath the olive trees. Briars caught his ankles but he didn't notice. The bed sheets next day were red from his scratches.

She asked for his address, but he had other things on his mind… Next morning he caught the early ferry from the island, spending hours in Skiathos before his flight; instead of saying goodbye to Loukia. Peter had grumbled from his bed and refused to go with him, annoyed at the unnecessary rush.

Alone in a taverna on the waterside in Skiathos, his hangover compounded his misery and he longed to be home. It would all be all right when he got home, and life returned to normal.

Only it wasn't. Ever since, her face had haunted him, her sad innocent eyes, her soft lips. He was consumed with guilt and regret. He should have left his number, taken hers. He knew he had to go back. He needed to tell her he was sorry.

"You want another Methos!" The waiter interrupted his thoughts, standing over him, pointing at his empty glass.

Greg stared at him. "You were here last year?" he asked.

The waiter nodded. "I here every year. My taverna." He grinned. "I was here last year too."

"From England." He rubbed his hands, nodding.

"You know Loukia?"

The innkeeper's face darkened. "You want another Methos?" The harsh tone made Greg flinch and he nodded.

The Greek beer was banged in front of him and Greg stared at the brown bottle, a film of icy condensation dripping slowly to form a pool at its base. He could see the man and his cronies muttering at the bar. Their eyes were fixed on him. He drank deeply.

He'd forgotten how strong the beer was. Settling his bill he set off across the track to his apartment. The sun was slipping slowly behind the mountains and he knew darkness would come suddenly. He felt woolly-headed and swore as he tripped over a stone.

As he reached the olive grove he shivered and stared into the dusky undergrowth. He heard nothing. No singing. Either he had imagined it or one of the locals had just been passing through. There was nothing sinister in singing. It was just… Loukia had sung to him, as they walked, a beautiful haunting Greek tune. The same tune he had heard earlier. But there was nothing unusual in that!

He heaved a sigh and struggled forward. The darkness now crept stealthily through the trees as the sun disappeared. Nearly there, round the next bend.

And then he heard a rustle through the blossoms and the poppies swayed, blood red in the evening glow and, unable to move forward, the lilting strains assailed his ears again. He peered through the creamy froths, swaying in the sudden breeze; he saw a light, a light dancing through the grasses to disappear behind the trees.

"Loukia?" he called, his voice quivering.

There was no reply and the music stopped as suddenly as it had begun. The grove was still and the poppies faded into dull red blurs as the sun finally left the island.

His heart pounding, his feet skidded into action and he ran. The bend loomed and then the blessed relief of lights. Bright lanterns, guiding him up the driveway of the apartments, welcoming lights on the steps and then he slammed his door. How normal everything looked. His clothes flung over a chair, the bed neatly made, the fridge humming.

Shaking slightly he filled the kettle. He should have remembered how strong the Greek beer was. He'd forgotten the hangovers, he'd forgotten that last night, his drunkenness.

Making a strong coffee, he subsided on the bed, trying to clear his mind. Befuddled, he gave up contemplation and crept beneath the cold sheets. Surprisingly, he slept.

The next morning, eating toast on his balcony under brilliant sunshine, he laughed at his fears. For goodness sake! What had he expected — Loukia to be sitting waiting for him? How could she, when she didn't even know he was coming?

No, Pavlos would have told her he was there and, hopefully, she would return to see him before he went home. There was still plenty of time. Today he would seek out Pavlos and get her telephone number. Positive action, positive thought. Buoyed with renewed confidence he headed for the village.

As he approached the olive grove he hesitated. The air was filled with the tinkle of goat bells and the sigh of laden branches in the breeze — no laughter. He stood for a moment. A goat path wended through the tall grasses, brown dust and pebbles denoting its meandering way. On impulse he followed it. Sunshine and reason had stilled his fear and he was determined to put his fantasies to rest.

Halfway down, he caught a glimpse of the goats in the neighbouring fenced grove. They raised their heads momentarily and glanced languidly at him, returning to their grazing, the bells entwined in their horns tinkling merrily.

Perhaps that was what he had heard, the laughter of the goat herd, feeding the animals, checking their presence. That made sense. Smiling at his own stupidity he strolled further until he came to a clearing. A fallen tree stretched across the trodden grass; wild flowers, lilac and yellow, mingled with the scarlet poppies. He stared around. Through the trees he could see a white house, nestling low but, he realised as he peered through the undergrowth, it was by the side of the lower road. Probably inhabited by the Greeks who owned the goats. There was no dwelling in the grove.

His mind at rest, he turned to head back and then his eyes caught a glimpse of red on a low olive branch. It was a silk scarf, snagged among the leaves, its redness coated in downy cream powder from the blossoms.

Pulling it free he fingered its softness. He had seen Greek girls with their black hair tied in such scarves. This one felt warm from the sun and, as he held it to his face, he smelt the pungent sweetness of the blossom.

Shaking it clean, he slipped it into his pocket. Whoever had seen to the goats, singing as she went, had lost her scarf. It wasn't Loukia, he accepted that, but the scarf, as he fingered it in the pocket of his shorts, reassured him that there was no ghost in the olive grove. His singing enchantress had been real!

Cheered, he returned to the track and, whistling the lilting Greek tune, followed the dusty road. Climbing the steep steps down to the village he took his usual seat in the taverna and ordered a Methos from the dour waiter.

"Has Pavlos been in today?"

The waiter shrugged.

Greg looked around. There were few customers, mainly tourists. Ordering a salad and bread, he settled down to wait.

Eventually, lulled into apathy by the beer and warmth, he headed back. A swim in the pool and then he would shower and return in the evening.

He was unprepared for the song that broke through his dullness as he passed the familiar olive grove; unprepared for the anger that coursed through his veins, ignited by alcohol.

How dare she! Not only had she frightened him half to death, she had wasted his valuable time, when he could have been searching for Loukia. He'd show her…

Stumbling off the track he headed down the path, his legs catching thistles and twigs. Unheeding of the scratches his anger coursed through him, red-hot in his veins, his brain exploding with rage. He pulled the red scarf from his pocket, clenching it between his fists until his nails bit his skin and his breath was harsh. He'd show her, he'd teach her to mess with him…

The singing became louder, insistent, as he closed in. She was there in the clearing. He could see a flash of red cloth, her dress as she moved.

Bursting through the undergrowth he gave a roar of triumph as he saw her face, smiling. For a moment anger blurred his vision, her slim vision alone; and then he stopped, breathing hard and his eyes wavered at he looked around. His hands unclenched and he brushed the sweat from his face. Confused now, he took a faltering step backwards, uneasiness creeping round the edges of his mind.

Perched on the gnarled black branch was Pavlos, his arm resting on the girl's shoulder. She smiled provocatively as she leaned against his legs and tossed her long hair, singing softly now, he lips barely moving as the words sighed to a hum. Greg fingered the red scarf and her eyes were amused as she watched him.

Several Greek men were lounging in the grasses; their eyes narrow as they watched him approach. Their fingers were idly picking the heads off the scarlet poppies. In the distance echoed the mournful call of peacocks.

"Pavlos," Greg smiled nervously, "I've been looking for you. I was going to ask you for Loukia's number, to contact her, tell her I was here…" His voice tailed off as Pavlos slowly slid to the ground, his eyes ice-slits in his grim face.

"Ah, Loukia…"

Greg shifted uneasily. The girl stopped singing. Pavlos halted inches from Greg, his eyes, deadly cold, raking his face. The breeze seemed to hold its breath, waiting in the silence.

And then Pavlos spoke quietly, calmly: "My sister was fifteen. You raped her."

Greg flinched. "No…" His voice shuddered through the blossoms and the grasses rustled as the men scrambled to their feet.

"She was left with child…"

"A baby?" Greg whispered, horror in his eyes.

"You should have contacted her. She waited." The words were chilling, precise.

"I didn't have her number… I've come back… "Greg was gabbling. "Just tell me where she is?" he implored.

"She walked into the sea." Pavlos' eyes were black steel above his twisted mouth.

Terror infiltrated Greg's senses and slipped icily through his bones.

The girl took the scarf from his limp fingers and began to braid it through her hair as she turned away, singing softly.

He swung round, but they had encircled him. Linking arms they crept forwards, smiling.